Dying For Danish

Leighann Dobbs

Other Works By Leighann Dobbs

Lexy Baker
Cozy Mystery Series
* * *

Killer Cupcakes
Dying For Danish
Murder, Money, & Marzipan
3 Bodies and a Biscotti
Brownies, Bodies & Bad Guys

Blackmoore Sisters
Cozy Mystery Series
* * *

Dead Wrong

Contemporary
Romance
* * *

Reluctant Romance
Forbidden Desires
Physical Attraction
Passionate Vengeance
Second Chances
Sweet Escapes (short story compilation)

----

*Dobbs "Fancytales"
Regency Romance Fairytales Series*
* * *

*Something In Red
Snow White and the Seven Rogues*

You can see all of Leighann's books at her website:
http://www.leighanndobbs.com

This is a work of fiction. None of it is real.
All names, places, and events are products of the author's imagination. Any resemblance to real names, places, or events are purely coincidental, and should not be construed as being real.

Dying For Danish
Copyright © 2012
Leighann Dobbs
http://www.leighanndobbs.com
All Rights Reserved.

No part of this work may be used or reproduced in any manner, except as allowable under "fair use," without the express written permission of the author.
10 9 8 7 6 5 4 3 2 1

Chapter One	7
Chapter Two	16
Chapter Three	28
Chapter Four	38
Chapter Five	44
Chapter Six	51
Chapter Seven	58
Chapter Eight	67
Chapter Nine	82
Chapter Ten	94
Chapter Eleven	102
Chapter Twelve	111
Chapter Thirteen	126
Chapter Fourteen	138
Chapter Fifteen	146

Chapter Sixteen	151
Chapter Seventeen	157
Chapter Eighteen	172
Epilogue	185
Lexy's Danish Pastry Recipe	189
A Note From The Author	197

Chapter One

Lexy felt her stomach flutter as she approached the massive oak door. Balancing a huge glass tray loaded with artfully stacked towers of lemon, cheese and strawberry Danish pastries in one hand she teetered up the steps on the spikes of her Jimmy Choo stilettos.

She still felt a bit intimidated by the large house even though she had been there twice before. The elegant Victorian, owned by the absurdly wealthy Toliver family for the entire one hundred and fifty years of its existence, had bragging rights of being the biggest house in their little town.

She shifted the weight of the tray onto her shoulder, careful not to tip it. The Danish were part of the setup for a morning brunch - a fancy affair to celebrate the upcoming wedding of aging family patriarch Xavier Toliver. The catering job could give a big boost to her little bakery business and she wanted everything to go perfectly.

Lexy took a deep breath. She grabbed the cold brass door knocker, rapping it against the plate to announce her arrival. Instead of the expected sound of footsteps coming to the door, she heard the squeak of hinges. The door swung open on it's own, beckoning her inside.

"Hello?" she ventured. *Maybe they're all busy getting ready and left it open so I could let myself in?*

Lexy pushed the door wider taking a tentative step into the marble foyer.

"Hello...it's me, Lexy Baker from the Cup and Cake." No answer. Lexy shrugged. *Better get to work.* She shifted the tray so the palm of her hand would steady it and bear most of the weight. Proceeding forward she made her way through the foyer to the great hall which led to the kitchen. Hollow clacking sounds from her heels on the cold tile bounced off the oak paneled walls.

The hallway opened up into the expansive kitchen. Even though the house was old, the kitchen was modernized - a showcase of gleaming granite and oak.

"Is anyone here? I have the pastries."

Lexy entered the kitchen. Looking for the best place to set the Danish, her eyes scanned the room, then settled on a pair of long tables covered in white cloths which had been placed by the palladium windows.

She skirted round the massive kitchen island, heading towards the tables. Something sticking out from behind the breakfast bar caught her eye. *Were those feet?*

She took a few steps over to get a closer look. They *were* feet - well dressed feet wearing the latest Steve Madden pumps laying at an impossible angle on the floor.

Lexy knew something was very wrong, she wanted to run, but her body seemed to have other ideas and it stepped closer to the feet. Against her will, her head craned around the corner.

Crash!

Lexy felt sharp pinches on her ankles, saw Danish pastries bouncing off the floor. She heard a loud, high scream that wouldn't stop. It took her a few minutes to realize the scream was coming from her.

***

The rough texture of crisp linen scratched against Lexy's cheek. Strong hands rubbed her back. She wasn't sure how long she had stood there screaming or whose hands were soothing her. Apparently the owner of those hands had a soothing voice to match and it was murmuring in her ear. It felt good. She wanted to just forget about everything else and melt into the crisp linen. But she couldn't.

Lexy turned away from the shirt. Her stomach lurched. Her breath caught sharply in her throat. She felt dizzy, but forced herself to look. In front of her, the kitchen was a sticky mess of Danish pastry, glass and blood. Yep, blood. The blood came from the body which had been attached to those designer clad feet - the body of Chastine Johnson, the fiancee of Xavier Toliver. She lay on her side on the kitchen floor, the blood apparently coming out of the big hole in her chest. A stab wound, Lexy guessed, although she'd never actually seen one in real life.

"Don't look." The murmurer tried to pull her head back to his chest. Lexy looked up. Concerned ice blue eyes looked back at her.

"Who are you?" she asked, pushing herself away reluctantly. Her eye started to twitch a bit at the corner. She put her finger up to it, mashing her lower lid in an effort to get the twitching to stop.

"Blake Toliver...and you are?" He held out his hand. Lexy reciprocated, her small hand disappearing inside his large one. The handshake was warm and firm. It felt rather pleasant despite the gruesome circumstances.

"I'm Lexy Baker. I own the Cup and Cake Bakery. I was delivering pastries for the brunch when I found..." She nodded in the direction of the body, letting her voice trail off. Ripping her glance away from the dead woman, she turned her attention back to Blake. She knew from what she had heard around town that Xavier Toliver had two sons. Blake was one of them, but she'd thought he would be older considering his father was well into his seventies.

Apparently Xavier had waited until later in life to become a father. The outcome wasn't half bad. Blake looked to be a few years older than Lexy. He was tall, about six feet and broad shouldered. Black curly hair framed a handsome face providing a perfectly, delicious contrast to his ice blue eyes. Lexy might have felt all tingly and hot if there hadn't been a body laying five feet away...and if she wasn't involved with someone...sort of.

She spun around at the sound of heavy boots coming up behind her. In front of her stood another tall, dark and handsome man. *The other son.* But where Blake was all charm and smiles, this one seemed dark and moody with black close cut hair and dark brown, stormy eyes.

Lexy held out her hand to make friends. "I'm Lexy Baker..."

"I heard you introduce yourself to my brother." He ignored her hand which Lexy let dangle foolishly in the air until the onset of another eye twitch caused her to grind it into her eye again.

"This is my brother Bronson," Blake interjected. "I apologize for his bad manners, he can be such a caveman sometimes."

Bronson ignored the remark. "I called 911 - the police should be here any minute." Sirens wailed in the distance as if to verify the statement.

"Shall we go in the other room, it's a bit unpleasant in here. We probably shouldn't be milling about the crime scene anyway." Blake put his hand on the small of Lexy's back propelling her down the hall. Lexy cast a look back over her shoulder marveling at how easy it was to get used to looking at a dead body - just minutes ago she was a screaming mess and now she could look over there with barely a tummy twinge.

Blake steered her inside a lavishly decorated room. He nodded towards a blue velvet antique tufted wing back chair motioning for her to sit while he moved behind a wet bar.

He grabbed a couple of ice cubes with silver tongs and dropped them into a short glass, the cubes made clinking sounds as they hit the bottom. Choosing a crystal decanter from the sideboard, he pulled off the top and filled a couple of fingers worth of smokey amber liquid from the decanter into the glass which he held up towards Lexy.

"Drink?"

Lexy shook her head. *Kind of early in the morning for drinks, isn't it?*

Blake looked over at Bronson who leaned against the doorframe, not quite in the room but not quite out of it either.

"Too early for you, Bronnie?"

Bronson just stared back.

Lexy couldn't help but notice a strange dynamic between the brothers which made her feel a bit uncomfortable. Their behavior towards each other wasn't the only thing that set her on edge. The thing that she found most odd was it appeared that neither of the brothers seemed too surprised...or upset...that a murder had just happened right in their own kitchen.

Chapter Two

Blake was only a couple of sips into his drink when the wail of sirens reached annoyingly loud decibels, then suddenly cut off announcing the arrival of the Brook Ridge Police Department.

The others went into the hall to greet them. Lexy stayed back hidden in the room, biding her time before she had to face *him. Maybe he wouldn't be the one to investigate this?*

For a moment she felt hope, or was it disappointment? She wasn't sure which, and didn't have much time to explore her feelings before a familiar voice came booming through the house. Detective Jack Perillo.

Lexy had met Jack earlier in the summer when her ex boyfriend had been poisoned with cupcake tops from her bakery. Jack had been the lead investigator in the murder. Lexy had been a suspect - her bakery had been closed down. In order to clear herself, she had been forced to do some investigating of her own causing their paths to cross under a variety of circumstances.

The two had a strong attraction to each other from the start. After the case was over, they had started dating. Everything was going great - they had become very close over the past several months. Lexy was even entertaining thoughts of Jack being *'the one'*.

Until a couple of weeks ago when Jack mysteriously stopped calling and answering her calls. All she had gotten in the past week and a half were a couple of unromantic text messages. It didn't help matters that Jack was her neighbor - she had a clear view of his house from her kitchen window allowing her to see his comings and goings whenever she chose.

Lexy had become so angry at the non responsive detective, she had shut her kitchen blinds refusing to open them. *She didn't care what Detective Jack Perillo was doing or who he was doing it with!*

The last person Lexy wanted to see was Jack, but it didn't seem like she had much of a choice now. Fortifying herself with a deep breath, she marched into the hallway, hoping she didn't react like a silly female and get all emotional. Having a fight with your sometimes boyfriend at the scene of a murder hardly seemed like proper etiquette.

Lexy turned the corner into the foyer. She stood in the entryway, her petite five foot one inch frame dwarfed by the much larger detectives and Toliver boys.

Against her will, her eyes immediately sought out Jack. He looked over at her, his warm honey brown eyes registering surprise - a smile forming on the corners of his lips. Lexy's stomach flip flopped, her mind whirling with a dizzying array of emotions which had nothing to do with discovering a dead body less than an hour ago - excitement, nervousness, lust and, most strongly...anger.

"Lexy!" Jack seemed genuinely happy to see her which added another emotion to her repertoire - confusion.

***

Jack looked across the foyer at Lexy. Her simple tee shirt and jeans showed off her curvy, petite figure. His heart swelled at the sight of her shoulder length mink brown hair pulled back in a pony tail made her bright green eyes seem even bigger than usual. Jack pulled his thoughts back to the matter at hand before things other than his heart started to swell.

"What are you doing here?" *What was she doing here?* Jack looked around at the Toliver boys - tall, rich and handsome. He felt an uncustomary pang of jealousy stab him in the chest. Then he realized he was being ridiculous. He was sure she wasn't there socially because after all, *they* were dating pretty seriously. Jack didn't think Lexy was the type to have another boyfriend on the side.

Suddenly Jack realized he had been so wrapped up in his latest case that he hadn't talked to Lexy in several days...maybe even weeks.

"I was delivering pastries here this morning."

Jack felt a surge of relief.

"She discovered the body." Blake offered.

"Speaking of which," one of the detectives piped in, "Can you show us where it is?"

Blake led the group to the kitchen. The team immediately sprang into action. In a matter of minutes, the kitchen resembled a scene from CSI.

After inspecting the body, Jack turned his attention to the Toliver brothers who were standing off to the side next to Lexy.

"Are you the sons of the deceased?"

Blake snorted out a laugh. "Hardly," he pointed over at the body. "Chastine Johnson was going to be our new step mommy - our dad was marrying her next week."

Jack felt his eyebrows rise. Neither one of them looked too upset the marriage would never happen.

"So, you're the Toliver sons then? Blake and Bronson, is it?"

Blake nodded. "I'm Blake," then pointed to his brother, "and this is Bronson."

"Do you both live here?"

"Yes," Blake answered for both of them.

"And you were home this morning?"

They both nodded.

"Who was present when the body was discovered?"

Lexy raised her hand. "Just me."

Jack signaled to his long haired, lanky partner, John Darling, who was bending over the body pointing out something to one of the technicians.

John looked over at them, his eyebrows arching when he noticed Lexy. "Hey Lexy, what are you doing here?"

"She discovered Ms. Johnson." Jack explained. "Maybe you could get a statement from Blake and Bronson Toliver. I'll take Lexy's."

John nodded, turning his attention on the Toliver brothers.

Jack pulled Lexy over into a private corner. "Are you OK? It must have been awful for you finding her like that." He reached out for her, pulling her into a soothing hug.

It was like hugging a stiff board. Jack realized he had been a bit selfish lately - wrapped up in his latest case he hadn't made any time for Lexy, thinking that she would just automatically understand. A pang of regret ripped through him. He pulled her even closer, hoping he hadn't ruined things with her by being so dedicated to his job.

***

Lexy felt a rush of emotions. The morning had been stressful. It felt good to have Jack's strong arms around her. She let herself relax into his embrace for a few seconds. She thought she heard him whisper "I'm sorry."

Then, Lexy remembered why she was mad at him. She pushed herself away, wriggling out of his arms. The past two weeks she had felt hurt and anger at Jack's lack of attention. She didn't need him coming to the rescue now.

She looked up at him, her heart clenching at the look of confusion in his eyes. "I'm fine," she managed to say.

Lexy watched him take a well worn notebook and pencil out of his pocket. "I'll have to ask you a few questions..."

"Of course."

"What time did you arrive here?"

Lexy bit the inside of her lip, trying to think back through the timeframe of the morning. She had left the bakery at around 8:10, making the trip to the mansion in fifteen minutes easy.

"Around 8:25," she answered.

"Who was here?"

"It was the strangest thing, no one was here. I knocked on the door and it swung open on its own. I had a big tray of Danish, so I brought them in."

Lexy didn't like the way Jack's brow furrowed. *Surely, he wasn't doubting her story?* She noticed with annoyance that her eye was starting to twitch again. She made an effort not to poke at it with her finger.

"And you didn't think it was odd no one was around? You just walked right in?"

"Yes, I did think it was odd but I just figured they were all getting ready for the party. They knew I was coming so I just thought they left the door open so I could find my own way in without disturbing them."

Jack nodded, scratching something in his notebook.

"So you were delivering food for some party - how do you know these people?"

"Nans knows Xavier Toliver from her younger days. She helped me get the catering job for their whole wedding shindig." Lexy said, wondering what Nans, her grandmother, was going to think of all this.

"Speaking of Xavier Toliver...where is he?" Jack asked, looking around the room.

Lexy's brows knit together. "I haven't seen him yet this morning."

Jack turned to walk back to the other room, motioning for her to stay put. Naturally she did no such thing. Something about the body had been nagging at her, and she wanted to go back to take a peek.

Lexy slipped around the edges of the kitchen stopping near where Chastine lay on the floor. She felt a twinge looking at her, but she couldn't say she was sad Chastine was dead. The woman had been quite beautiful but had a nasty disposition that made it impossible to like her. A sparky blonde of about 45 she was, of course, much younger than

Xavier. Rumor had it she was only marrying him for his money and Lexy didn't doubt it was true.

The woman had expensive taste and it would take all of Tolivers millions to keep her in style. The few times Lexy had seen her, she'd been dressed in designer outfits wearing expensive jewelry. There was one pin Lexy had admired in particular. *The pin!* That's what had been nagging at her. Chastine always wore an expensive pin- a daisy with a very unusual canary yellow cushion cut diamond in the center, but Lexy hadn't noticed the pin on the body this morning.

Lexy shuffled closer to the body. Slowly she bent over to look at the lapels of the fuchsia silk shirt. She felt her breath catch in her throat - the right lapel had a tear in it, as if someone had ripped the pin right off her.

"Lexy?" Jack's voice interrupted her from across the room. She straightened abruptly wobbling on her high heels, almost toppling onto the body.

She looked over at him, eyebrows raised.

"We're not quite done here." He said, motioning for her to join him.

Lexy picked her way over to him. He was standing with John and Blake. Blake was explaining that his father normally slept in so he wouldn't be around this time of morning. He had sent Bronson upstairs to wake him. Suddenly the air was split with an anguished wail.

"Looks like Bronson has given Dad the news." Blake said raising his glass to his lips and swigging down the rest of his drink.

Chapter Three

"What took so long? The rest of the pastries have been ready for an hour!" Cassie, Lexy's assistant and best friend, stood in the doorway to the kitchen, hands on hips, her pink hair ruffled up into an angry spike.

Lexy blew out a breath, "You won't believe what happened!"

Cassie lifted her eyebrows in response. "What?"

"Chastine Johnson's been murdered!" Lexy blurted out. She watched Cassie's face run through a gamut of emotions - surprise, confusion then disbelief.

"No, that can't be....what will we do with all these pastries?" She spread her arms in the direction of the kitchen which was loaded to the brim with baked goods - cinnamon buns, eclairs, banana and pumpkin breads, brownies and Lexy's signature pastry -cupcake tops loaded with creamy frosting.

Lexy stopped short. She hadn't considered that. What *would* they do with all the pastry? What would happen to her big catering job now that there would be no wedding?

Feeling light headed, Lexy plopped down in one of the tall kitchen chairs. She took a deep breath. The familiar scent of flour, sugar and cinnamon acted as a soothing balm and kicked her brain into gear.

"I hadn't thought about that." She tapped her front teeth with long, red nails. "With Chastine dead, there won't be any wedding...*and* I spent the money from the job on the new kitchen equipment."

The girls looked around the bakery kitchen. Brand new appliances gleamed in every corner - commercial ovens, mixers and a walk in refrigerator had just been installed to replace the old, used ones they had been making-do with.

Lexy had opened her bakery, *The Cup and Cake*, barely a year ago on a shoe string budget. A loan from her parents who had sold their home to travel the country in an RV had helped her buy what she needed, but she had to stretch each dollar and had only been able to afford older, used equipment. That equipment didn't work up to par and broke down quite a bit which made it harder to get the work done. New equipment would be more efficient and allow her to be more productive, which would make the bakery more profitable.

Her business had been growing nicely, but she wouldn't have been able to afford all new kitchen equipment if it wasn't for the Toliver's big catering job. If she lost all that money, she would have a hard time paying the equipment bill which would be coming any day now.

Lexy felt her stomach drop. Her business could be at risk if she didn't collect at least part of the payment - for several parties she'd already catered for him - including this mornings. Xavier had promised her the partial payment today, but considering the circumstances she doubted *that* would happen.

"We need to get whatever money we can from this job or we could be in big trouble." She said, feeling tears threaten.

"Jeez, Lexy, I'm not sure how you can do that...I mean you can't just breeze in on the day the guys fiancee gets murdered and present him with a bill."

"Yeah, that would be rude," Lexy agreed. "I couldn't do it, but I know someone who could. Can you hold down the fort here for a little while?"

Cassie nodded.

"Great - I'll be back in a bit." Lexy said, stuffing a raspberry scone into her mouth as she slid off her chair, grabbed her purse and ran out the back door.

***

Lexy whipped her yellow VW beetle into the first parking spot she found at the Brook Ridge Retirement Community. Her grandmother, or Nans as Lexy called her, had recently moved to the upscale community for retirees to be closer to friends and not have to worry about driving. She had given the old Craftsman style bungalow she lived in for most of her life to Lexy.

Lexy had called ahead to make sure Nans was around - with all her senior activities the woman could be impossible to get in touch with, but today Lexy had lucked out - Nans was waiting for her inside.

Breezing in through the large glass doors to the comfortably furnished lobby of the retirement center, her eyes scanned the room. They found Nans at a round table with her three closest friends. The four of them could usually be found at that table, talking, having coffee and, as Lexy had discovered earlier in the summer, solving murders with the help of their iPads.

Lexy rushed over, swallowing Nans in a big hug. "Morning ladies," she addressed the group. Ida, Ruth and Helen murmured greetings. They looked ready for anything in their polyester print shirts and fresh blueish gray perms.

"I can see something is bothering you," Nans stated, her intelligent green eyes studying Lexy's face.

Lexy took a deep breath. "I was delivering food to the Toliver's this morning for a brunch and I discovered Chastine Johnson's body in the kitchen."

The ladies gasped, then leaned forward. "Murdered?" Ida asked with a gleam in her eye.

Lexy nodded.

"How?" Ruth chimed in.

"Well, I'm no expert on bodies, but it looked like she'd been stabbed in the chest."

The four women exchanged excited glances. Lexy was afraid this might happen. At the beginning of the summer when her ex, Kevin, had been poisoned, Lexy had turned to Nans for comfort and discovered the four women had an odd hobby. They solved murders. They even had a name for themselves - *The Ladies Detective Club*.

They didn't go out roaming the streets in trench coats - well, not usually. They preferred to stay in the retirement center gathering clues from the internet which they accessed through their iPads. They had been instrumental in helping her find Kevin's killer but she didn't need help solving a murder right now, she only wanted to collect the money for the catering jobs she'd done for Xavier Toliver.

"Tell us everything you know about it." Nans demanded.

"Nans, I didn't come here to try to solve the murder, I just wanted to ask you a teensy, tiny favor." Lexy held her hand up, her index finger and thumb a tiny space apart.

"Oh, anything for you dear," Nans said. "I'll do whatever you want...right after you tell us everything you know about the murder."

With a sigh, Lexy pulled out a chair, flopping into it. The four women leaned in towards her. Lexy told them about how the door had swung open when she knocked, how she had let herself in and discovered the body in the kitchen.

"No one was there?" Helen asked, the wrinkles on her forehead doubling.

"What was she wearing?" Ida asked.

"Did you see the murder weapon?" Ruth added.

Lexy bit her lower lip trying to remember. "Come to think of it, I didn't see the murder weapon...I don't know if they found it."

The women nodded knowingly.

"That's the first thing you should look for." Helen said.

Lexy held up her hands. "No, no...I'm not trying to find the killer on this one, ladies."

Trying to ignore the looks of disappointment on their faces, she went on, "I do have one little problem though."

Nans cocked her head to one side, "Go on, dear."

"As you know, the Toliver's hired me to cater all the events leading up to and including the wedding. Obviously there will be no wedding now, but I desperately need to collect at least the money for what I have done so far. I was supposed to get paid half now and the rest after the wedding, but with the murder now I'm not sure how to collect my money." She looked at Nans, "That's the favor I wanted, I was hoping you could go over there with me...you know...to give your condolences to Xavier and maybe give him a hint about the payment."

"Of course, Xavier and I have been great friends since grade school so I *should* go over and give my condolences. He must be crushed...you know, he really did care for her. We can go right now, if you want."

Lexy looked at her watch, several hours had passed since she was last at the mansion which gave Xavier a bit of time to process the information. She stood up, pushing her chair in. "Now would be perfect."

Ida, Ruth and Helen were already pulling out their iPads - presumably to *Google* the Tolivers and start their investigation.

As Lexy made her way across the lobby to the door with Nans she heard Ida yell out after them, "Don't forget to question anyone who is there, inspect the crime scene and bring us back some clues!"

Chapter Four

Lexy approached the big oak door with butterflies in her stomach for the second time that day. Unlike earlier, though, the door didn't open on its own when she tapped the brass knocker.

After a couple of seconds, it did swing inward revealing Blake. His face registered surprise when he saw Lexy. "What brings you here again? Not that it isn't a pleasure to see you," he said, his eyes making a round trip down her body then back up to her face.

"I think you know my grandmother, Mona Baker?" she gestured towards Nans.

Blake's eyebrows shot up. "Of course, Mona...how are you?

"Oh, fine dear. Lexy told me about Chastine. I've come to give my condolences to your father. How is he holding up?"

Blake opened the door wider, inviting them inside. "He's doing as well as can be expected. I think a visit from you might cheer him up."

He ushered Nans and Lexy into a large library. She hadn't seen this room on any of her previous visits. It was impressive. Oak bookcases filled with leather bound books lined the walls from floor to ceiling. The floor was covered in a sumptuous oriental rug with rich red and blue colors. It smelled of old books and cigars.

A large fireplace sat at one end of the room flanked by two leather chairs on either side of an expensive looking tufted leather couch. Xavier Toliver reclined in one of the chairs at the end of the room, a box of tissues by his side. His eyes were red rimmed. He looked haggard and older than his seventy-eight years.

Nans rushed to Xavier's side. "Xavier, I just heard about Chastine - I'm so sorry!"

"Thank you Mona, it's been such a shock." His voice broke on the last word. He dabbed at his eyes with a tissue.

Nans patted his knee. "I know you really cared for her, Xavvy," she soothed.

"I don't know who could have done such an awful thing to such a lovely girl...and right in my own kitchen!"

Lexy heard a snort come from behind her, she turned to see Blake.

"Dad, it could have been plenty of people. Chastine pissed off lots of folks."

Nans turned to Blake. Lexy could practically see the wheels in her mind turning with the hint of a good clue.

"Who could she have made that angry?" Nans asked, her face a mask of innocence.

"Well, most of the staff hated her, she treated Dad's friends rudely, anyone who ever waited on her at a store or restaurant..." He let his voice trail off indicating the suspect list could be very long.

"But, surely, most of those people wouldn't go to such lengths." Nans said.

Blake shrugged in response leaving them to sit in silence, each of them contemplating who might have been mad enough to kill Chastine.

Hushed, angry voices drifted in from the hallway. Everyone turned towards the noise. Lexy strained in her seat to hear what they were saying.

"...not leaving... care ... do with it." The last words were spoken sharply, accentuated by the clicking of high heels hurrying away from them down the hall. Bronson appeared in the doorway, his eyes growing wide when he saw all four of the occupants of the room staring in his direction.

"Who was that?" Blake asked Bronson.

Lexy thought she saw Bronson's face grow red under his dark complexion. "Oh, just Candice...she was getting some of her things out of Chastine's office."

Blake looked at his brother sideways. "Sounded like there was more to it than that..." he said under his breath. A warning look from Bronson caused him to snap his mouth shut and go back to staring at the ice cubes in his drink.

"Who is Candice?" Nans asked.

"Candice is...was...Chastine's personal assistant." Xavier said.

Lexy and Nans exchanged a knowing look. *The personal assistant of the murder victim trading angry words with the son?* That was a clue the Ladies Detective Club will love to hear about.

Nans looked back at Xavier. "I don't want to take up any more of your time, I just wanted to come to give my condolences - and to thank you for hiring Lexy to do all your catering. Speaking of which, we were wondering if Lexy should bill you right away for the remainder...considering..."

"Bill?" Xavier threw his hands up dramatically, "I couldn't even think about paying a bill now. Not while the murderer of my Schmoopie is still running around loose. I can't consider such mundane activities until *that* person is behind bars!" He said, then collapsed in a torrent of tears giving Lexy and Nans their cue to make a hasty retreat.

Chapter Five

"I'm sorry, dear," Nans looked over at Lexy from the passenger seat, "Xavier was so distraught I couldn't push him about paying you."

"That's OK, Nans. I'll figure something out to keep my cash flow on the positive side."

"Oh, you won't have to worry. The Ladies Detective Club will get right on it, and we'll have the murderer figured out in no time. Then you can get your bill paid!"

"That's exactly what I was afraid you'd say." Lexy poked at her eye, which had started twitching again.

"Oh now, come on...we've had some good successes - even Jack admitted we helped him in a few cases." She looked at Lexy sideways. "Speaking of Jack, are you two still a hot item?"

Lexy felt her cheeks grow warm. *Were they still an item?* She didn't know the answer and had more pressing problems to think of. Luckily, they had arrived at the Brook Ridge Retirement Center so she could avoid the question by changing the subject.

"Here we are...we might as well go and fill the ladies in." She opened her car door and climbed out, waiting for Nans to do the same.

They headed for the lobby. Lexy wasn't the least bit surprised to find Ida, Ruth and Helen waiting for them at the usual table, their iPads at the ready. The three ladies peppered them with questions as soon as they sat down.

"What did you find out?"

"Did you get a look at the crime scene?"

"How is Xavvy holding up?"

"Whats wrong with your eye?"

Nans filled them in on Xavier and the argument they heard in the hall.

"Xavier was so upset when I asked about paying Lexy's bill that I never got a chance to look at the murder scene."

"We'll need to look into this Candice person." Ruth clicked on her iPad. "Do you know her last name?"

Nans and Lexy shook their heads to the obvious disappointment of the others.

"Lexy," Helen said, scooting her chair in, "Do you remember what the murder scene looked like?"

Lexy thought back to the morning. "There was a lot of blood...and Chastine was laying on her side...I don't remember much else."

"I can help you remember. Sit, back and relax. Close your eyes."

Lexy did as she was told.

Helen continued in a calm soothing voice. "Picture yourself walking into the kitchen. What do you hear? What do you smell?"

Lexy pictured the kitchen in her minds eye. "The clock is ticking but otherwise it is very quiet. I smell pastries...and copper."

"Do you see the body, how is it positioned?"

"I saw her feet first - I noticed the shoes because they were a pair of Steve Maddens I've had my eye on. The rest of her was hidden by the counter. Then I peeked around and saw all the blood."

"Go on, what did the body look like? Remember, you're safe here with us."

Lexy felt like she had been transported back in time. She could see Chastine perfectly.

"She was laying on her side, the blood was coming from a big gap in her chest. Really big. Her hair was perfectly coiffed. She had on a blue skirt and fuchsia shirt. They looked great together and she had all her nice jewelry - her bracelet, rings, earrings...wait! Her pin!" Lexy's eyes popped open.

"Yes?" Ruth prompted.

"She always wore a gorgeous pin. I'd admired it several times because it had an unusual stone in it - a canary yellow cushion cut diamond. The pin was missing...a hole ripped in the shirt where it should have been!"

The women exchanged excited glances. Ruth tapped something into the notepad app on her iPad.

"That was great, Lexy. It could be a valuable clue which might help us find the killer." Helen said.

"Great!" Lexy felt happy about helping, then her eyes narrowed with suspicion. "Wait a minute, did you just hypnotize me?"

Ruth nodded. "Yes, that skill comes in handy for many things. I can also help you get rid of that annoying eye twitch."

"You can?" Lexy's finger went up to her eye. She would have to consider that, the eye twitch *was* getting pretty annoying.

Ida clapped her hands softly. "Lets get back on track here, we don't want the trail to grow cold!"

Nans turned to Lexy. "Lexy, you'll need to do some digging. Find out about this Candice person - her last name and what her relationship is with that Toliver boy. See if Chastine had any enemies. Maybe you could go back there and poke around for the murder weapon?"

"Make a list of anyone you think is a suspect - don't forget to include anyone who had means, motive and opportunity." Ida instructed, punctuating each word with a shake of her finger.

"Right." Lexy nodded, feeling like she was getting a homework assignment from her grade school teacher.

"We'll get to work here researching the backgrounds of the suspects and poking around pawn shops to see if the pin surfaces," Nans said.

The ladies went to pawn shops? Lexy stared at them, picturing the four women in trench coats launching a clandestine trip to the seedy section of town to canvas the pawn shops.

"Well, don't sit there - get a move on!" Nans startled Lexy out of her fantasy. She jumped up, said her goodbyes and started towards the door.

"Oh, and find out when the wake is," Nans called after her, "I think the Ladies Detective Club is due for a little field trip!"

Chapter Six

"Thank God you're back - I've been swamped!" Cassie greeted Lexy as she rushed in the back door to the bakery.

"Sorry," she said, grabbing a vintage pink and brown striped apron from the rack and securing it around her waist. "I took Nans over to the Toliver's to see if we could get the payment for all this." She spread her arms to indicate all the pastries they had made for the brunch that day.

"I can see by your face that you didn't."

"Nope. Xavier said he couldn't think of paying bills while his fiancees murderer was loose."

Lexy saw Cassie's face fall. "Don't worry, we'll figure something out. Maybe I can get the equipment vendor to put us on a payment plan. In the meantime, let's get these goodies out into the cases so people can buy them."

Lexy carried a tray of whoopee pies towards the gleaming glass display cases in the front. On the side that faced the street she had setup a small area with coffee urns and tables for people to sit while they sipped coffee and ate pastry. Lexy's passion was baking in the kitchen, but she loved this part of her bakery the best because it was where she could interact with customers and show off her creations.

She inhaled the aroma of fresh brewed coffee mixed with the sugary smell of baking while she gazed out the window at the scenic waterfall across the street. She had been lucky to get this storefront because it had a wonderful view of Brook Ridge Falls, the waterfall the town was named after.

Fall was just starting and this was her favorite time of year. The waterfall's beauty was highlighted by the color of the turning leaves and, for a moment, she was captivated by the scene. She was just about to start loading the case when she saw a familiar figure stroll by. *Christian!*

Christian owned the beauty salon *Cliptomania* which was two doors down from Lexy's bakery and he knew everything about everybody.

"Cassie, there goes Christian - get him in here so we can pump him for information about the Tolivers!"

Cassie grabbed a Danish and ran out the door. Lexy watched through the window as she lured the young man into the bakery. Today, he was sporting an orange tipped blonde, spikey hairdo which complimented his orange bowling shirt and matching orange basketball sneakers.

Christian loved desserts. Lexy had his favorite, a German chocolate brownie oozing with sweet caramel topping, already on a plate. His eyes lit up when he saw her holding it out to him.

"For moi?" he said pointing at himself in an exaggerated manner.

Lexy nodded. "We have an excess of baked goods." She spread her hands to indicate the loaded trays they had brought from the back room. "I was supposed to cater the party for the Tolivers today…and well…you heard what happened, right?"

"Heard about it? That's all they've been talking about in the shop this morning." He leaned in towards Lexy and lowered his voice. "Most people think she deserved it, she was a real *bee-ach*."

Lexy smiled to herself, she knew Christian couldn't resist good gossip. She took the opportunity to probe for more information.

"I heard the sons hated her, do you think one of them did it?"

"Bronson or Blake?" He asked pursing his lips. "I doubt either of those two would get their hands dirty with something like that."

Lexy saw him eyeing the cinnamon buns and she handed one over. Christian bit into it rolling his eyes in ecstasy. "Heaven!"

She grabbed a large bakery box and started filling it while she waited for him to finish chewing.

"So, who's the prime suspect according to the gossip mill?" she asked, reaching over the counter with a napkin to wipe a big glob of frosting from his lower lip.

"Well, Mandy Pinterman thinks it could have been someone from her past. Apparently Chastine was just as bitchy when she lived back in Texas. I heard she had some nasty business with an old boyfriend there." Christian screwed up his face. "But Xavier's old girlfriend, Trixie Waters, is a client too and she was mad as a hornet when Xavier dumped her for Chastine. She even said she was mad enough to kill…"

Lexy's eyes went wide. "Really? Do you think she could have done it?"

Christian looked down at the last bite of his cinnamon bun apparently considering Lexy's question. "You never know what people will do when pushed to their limits." He popped the last bite into his mouth, swallowing it almost without chewing.

"Well, I gotta get back to the shop - the afternoon rush will start and I have four cuts and three colors lined up."

"Oh, wait, I'll give you some pastries to take with you." Lexy indicated the box she was filling. "We have so many left over, I don't want them to go to waste." Not to mention the advertising opportunity with her bakery name on the box, she thought to herself.

She finished tying up the box and handed it across the counter.

"Thanks bunches!" Christian turned to leave, bouncing his way toward the door, the box held high.

"Oh, one other thing," Lexy called after him. "Do you know anything about Chastine's assistant, Candice? Did she get her hair done at your shop?"

Christian turned back to face Lexy. "She was a strange one. She came in with Chastine but never had anything done herself. Although she could have used it - she was plain as a door mouse, but some highlights and the right cut could have done wonders."

He paused, his eyebrows knitting together. "Then again, her dull hair must not have hurt her too much in the romance department, I saw her with Bronson Toliver once at dinner and they seemed pretty cozy." He wiggled his eyebrows at Lexy, opened the door and disappeared out onto the street.

Chapter Seven

"Looks like the big customer rush is over out there." Cassie appeared in the kitchen doorway startling Lexy into almost dropping the butter, sugar, flour, eggs and large bowl she was trying to balance in her arms.

"Oh, good. We need to get more cupcake tops made...if you can believe it with all these extra pastries." She settled the ingredients on the large prep island in the middle of the kitchen. "Did you hear what Christian said about the murder gossip?"

Cassie nodded, peeking into the oven to check on the batch of cupcakes Lexy had put in earlier.

"Of course, that's just idle chit-chat, but some of that gossip can have hidden clues." Lexy worked the butter and sugar together in a large stainless steel bowl.

"Definitely." Cassie said, grabbing a pair of oven mitts, she slid the steaming tray of cupcakes out of the oven.

"We have a lot of things to look into," Lexy said cracking an egg into the bowl with the butter and sugar mixture, then adding the milk and vanilla. She set the bowl under one of her new mixers, turned the machine on low then watched as the beaters did the job of blending the ingredients.

"Let's make a list." Cassie wiped her hands down on her 1950's cherry pattern apron then pulled a pen and paper out of a drawer.

"Well, first we need to find out if Chastine had any enemies." Lexy left the mixer, moving over to a rack of cooled cupcakes. Picking up a long icing spatula, she slid it across the top of the pan, expertly slicing off the cupcake tops.

"Then there's the little matter of finding the murder weapon, or even what, exactly it was."

"Candice's last name," Cassie said scrawling the note on the paper without looking up.

Lexy set the cupcake tops on a rack. Moving over to the mixer she turned it off, hefted the bowl, poured the batter into the little cups of a fresh cupcake pan and slid it into the oven.

"Oh, *and* Nans and the girls want to know when the wake is. It sounded like they all wanted to go." Lexy rolled her eyes eliciting a laugh from Cassie.

"Those old ladies sure are something," Cassie said, "ok, is that it? I have the list down here on paper. How do you propose we find all this stuff out?"

Lexy bit her lower lip while she assembled the ingredients for buttercream frosting - whipping cream, butter, confectioners sugar and vanilla extract.

"We might be able to find out about the murder weapon from the police," she said sneaking a look at Cassie.

"Well, you have an *in* with them don't you?" Cassie raised the first two fingers on each hand in the air wiggling them to punctuate the word *in*.

"Umm...I'm not so sure..." Lexy said softly, focusing on mixing the frosting to the right consistency.

Lexy saw Cassie's eyebrows go up making her eyebrow ring stick straight out. She ignored the look and focused her mind on trying to figure out how they could get their answers. The last thing she needed right now was to get distracted by thinking about Jack.

"I think we might need to take another trip over to the Tolivers to ask some questions." She put the frosting bowl down and armed herself with a spatula.

"How would we do *that*? I mean it's not like we run in the same social circles." Cassie moved over next to Lexy. The girls worked side by side scooping big dollops of frosting then spreading them in generous heaps on the cupcake tops. Since business was slow in the afternoon, they often worked together in the kitchen like this, taking turns manning the front room.

Lexy looked around the kitchen for a tray to put her newly frosted cupcake tops on. She didn't see any available. "Where are all the trays?"

"That's it!" Cassie clapped her hands. "You brought some trays over to the Toliver's already and they are still there. You can use *that* as an excuse to go over!"

"Brilliant! But what do you mean *I* can use that as an excuse? I'm not going over there by myself...I think you're going to need to come with me on this one."

Lexy glanced up over the top of the cupcake she was frosting, biting her cheek to keep from laughing at the horrified look on Cassie's face - her eyes wide and her mouth sputtering open and closed like a fish. Cassie had a problem with authority and abhored people with money. Lexy knew she wouldn't want to go to the Toliver's but she really needed someone else there to help her sort out what they told her.

The bell over the front door announced the arrival of a customer before Cassie could come up with an excuse. "Your turn." Lexy said, pointing to the doorway which led to the front of the bakery.

Cassie spun around heading for the front, fixing Lexy with an over the shoulder glare on her way out.

Lexy focused on frosting the cupcake tops. The sugary vanilla scent of the rich creamy frosting was so inviting she decided she needed a little snack. She brought the top she was frosting up to her lips. Biting in, she savored the burst of creamy sweetness. She rolled the bite around in her mouth - just enough chocolate cake to add some balance and an even amount of frosting for a silky texture. It was like heaven! She said a silent prayer of thanks that she could eat as many desserts as she wanted without gaining an ounce, then took another bite...and another.

Voices drifted in from the front of the bakery. She recognized Cassie and a male voice which sounded familiar. Lexy gulped down the rest of the cupcake top. Wiping the evidence from her lips, she poked her head out into the front to see who it was. To her surprise she saw Cassie leaning casually on the counter, a blush on her cheeks her face tilted coquettishly upwards at Jack's partner, detective John Darling. *Was he here on police business?*

Lexy ventured out front. "Hi John." She greeted the tall detective. He stood opposite Cassie, leaning in against the case. His medium brown, long curly hair pulled back in a neat pony tail, his black leather jacket a smart contrast to his faded jeans. Lexy had to admit he was looking good. No wonder Cassie was practically batting her eyelashes at him.

"Hi Lexy. I hope you are OK after this mornings excitement?" Lexy was touched at the genuine concern she saw in his hazel eyes.

"Oh, I'm fine, thanks."

"Good. I just came to corroborate your timeline with Cassie." He flipped open a small spiral notebook. "You told Jack that you arrived at the Toliver's around 8:25?"

Lexy thought back to the morning and nodded, wondering why Jack wasn't there to ask about it himself. *Was he avoiding her?*

"You came straight from the bakery?"

"Yep, I loaded up with pastries and went right over."

John looked at Cassie. "Do you remember what time she left the bakery this morning?"

Cassie wrinkled her brow. "I had gotten stuck in traffic, so I didn't make it here until about five past eight. Lexy left right after."

John nodded, looking down to consult his notebook. He flipped the book shut and put it in his pocket. Pushing himself away from the case, he backed up a few steps to leave.

"One other thing, do you guys have a seven inch serrated knife?"

Cassie and Lexy glanced at each other. "Was that the murder weapon?"

John nodded.

Lexy composed her face into a mask of innocence. "We have lots of knives here at the bakery...some seven inch ones but I'd have to look around the kitchen to find them."

"OK, well if you find one is missing, let me know." John backed away from the case nodding at the two girls before turning to saunter out the door.

Lexy snuck a peek over at Cassie to see her expression but the other girl was too busy ogling John's backside.

Lexy felt a nervous flutter start in her stomach. She did have a seven inch serrated knife and she knew *exactly* where it was. It was the knife she used to cut breads and pastries when she was catering a party like the Toliver's. Right now, it was...or had been...sitting on the catering table where she had put it when she was setting up in their kitchen two days earlier.

Chapter Eight

Lexy rolled over, plumping the pillow under her head, arching her back to stretch her petite frame under the covers. Reluctantly, she opened her eyes. Deep brown ones looked back at her adoringly from the other side of the pillow. Too bad they weren't Jack's.

Sprinkles, her dog, was laying opposite her in the bed, her head on the pillow gazing expectantly at Lexy.

Lexy couldn't help but smile, the little poodle and Shih-tzu mix always made her feel happy.

"Good morning, are you ready for breakfast?" She reached out to pet the dog's silky fur.

Sprinkles answered by leaping up and running circles on the bed which made Lexy giggle out loud.

Lexy swung her legs over the side of the bed and followed the dog downstairs. In the kitchen, she scooped food out of the stainless steel canister she kept on the counter, pouring it into Sprinkles's ceramic dog bowl.

Before she could stop herself, she lifted the corner of the window shade to peek at Jack's house. His truck wasn't in the driveway so he had either already gone to work or didn't come home at all. She hoped it was the former.

The sound of Sprinkles's nails clacking on the kitchen floor caught her attention. She bent down, placing the bowl on the floor much to Sprinkles delight. She watched the dog attack the food with the gusto of a starving lion.

Glancing at the clock, she felt a pang of anxiety. *Better get a move on.* She had decided she would let Haley, their part-time help, watch the bakery while she and Cassie went over to the Toliver's.

She ran through the living room, stopping only for a second to straighten out the pillows on the leather sectional. When Nans had moved to the retirement center, she had given Lexy the Craftsman style house which she had lived in most of her life.

She'd also left many of the furnishings. Lexy loved being surrounded by Nans things and she had made only a few changes, the leather couch being one of them. She had loved coming here to visit Nans as a little girl and it was still one of her favorite places to be.

She took the stairs two at a time and sprinted into the bedroom. Wrenching the closet doors open, her eyes scanned the racks searching for the perfect outfit. Something a little flirty might not be a bad idea if she was going to try to get the Toliver boys to open up to her. Then again, she had an idea where the murder weapon might be hidden and looking for it might involve getting dirty so she didn't want to wear anything too dressy.

She picked out her favorite pair of faded jeans that were tight in all the right places, paired it with a black crop top that was cut low and cropped perfectly so it revealed only a hint of skin when she stretched the right way and completed it with a pair of platform shoes that weren't too drastically tall.

After showering, she took the time to blow dry her shoulder length hair so she could wear it down instead of putting it up in the usual ponytail. The blow dryer made her brown hair fluffy and a bit wavy. She scrutinized herself in the mirror...what was missing? *Makeup!* She grabbed some taupe eyeshadow, applying it lightly to set off her green eyes, then swiped on eyeliner, mascara and frosty lip gloss. After approving the look in her full-length mirror she started downstairs, her platforms making clomping noises on the wooden treads.

In the kitchen, Lexy went straight to the fridge for breakfast. She pulled out a cheese Danish - left over from the Toliver pastries. She ate it standing over the sink, the sugary sweetness flooding into her bloodstream giving her a burst of energy for the morning's activities. Sprinkles watched from her dog bed, her eyes longingly following every crumb that dropped.

Wiping a smudge of frosting from her face with a napkin, Lexy threw Sprinkles a treat, grabbed her car keys and headed out to meet Cassie at the bakery.

***

Lexy tapped the large brass door knocker against the giant oak door of the Toliver mansion. She glanced over at Cassie who was standing rigidly with her arms crossed in front of her.

"Relax, they're not *that* bad you know." She said, ignoring the angry, sideways glare Cassie fixed on her out of the corner of her eye.

The door opened inward giving the girls a view of Blake Toliver looking rather handsome with a half buttoned shirt, his hair wet from a recent shower. He looked at Lexy appreciatively "Well well, well... our beautiful baker is back. To what do we owe this honor?"

Lexy awarded him with her most dazzling smile. "This is my assistant Cassie ... Cassie, this is Blake Toliver." Lexy waved her hands between the two of them. Blake stuck his hand out to shake Cassie's which she begrudgingly offered him, then looked back at Lexy one eyebrow raised.

"We came to collect the rest of our catering trays and other things. I left everything in the kitchen yesterday when..."

"Oh, right," he said, opening the door wider. " I think the police are all done in there, come on in."

He held the door open to let the girls walk through. They preceded him into the hall. Lexy cast a furtive glance backwards, to catch him staring at her jean clad backside. She gave him a little wink - not that she was flirting - she preferred to think of it as buttering him up for questioning.

They continued forward into the kitchen. Lexy was glad to see it had been cleaned up but the obvious area in the middle where Chastine's body had been was a reminder of what had happened just the day before.

"So, how are you all doing? Is your dad okay?" Lexy scanned the room while trying to encourage conversation. She saw her tablecloths, trays, chafing dishes and other assorted paraphernalia where she had left them on the tables but there was one item she didn't see - the seven inch serrated knife.

"Oh, Dad's okay. He was really broke up about Chastine, but Trixie came over to give her condolences. She seems to have lifted his spirits immensely."

"Trixie?" Lexy pretended not to know about Xavier's ex-girlfriend.

"Trixie was Dad's old girlfriend. Another gold digger - he seems to attract them." Blake shrugged. "Dad dumped her when Chastine came along."

Lexy raised an eyebrow and stepped a little bit closer to Blake who didn't seem to mind at all. "Oh really? She must've been mad when that happened."

"Madder than a nest full of hornets." He grinned, running his finger teasingly along the bottom of Lexy's crop top with a gleam in his eye.

Lexy swatted his hand away playfully letting out a little giggle. She knew she was flirting shamelessly but it wasn't that hard to flirt with Blake Toliver. He was rich and handsome - what more could a girl want? She could almost see herself wanting to get to know Blake better except for one thing - she was stuck on Jack Perillo.

"Do you think Trixie could have killed Chastine?" Lexy asked her face a mask of wide-eyed innocence.

Blake pursed his lips while apparently thinking about the question. "I'm not sure, anyone could have killed her because the back door was wide open."

Lexy swiveled her head over towards the back kitchen door. "It was?"

"Yep, I guess no one noticed it that morning, but the police asked us later who had opened the door. None of us had opened it. The killer could have been someone who just came in the back door - it could have been anyone off the street."

"But it probably wasn't," Lexy said. "Chances are it was someone who had it in for Chastine. Did she have any enemies?"

Blake snorted out a laugh. "Enemies? The question should be did she have any friends. She made an enemy out of almost everyone who came into contact with her."

"What about you and Bronson, you must have liked her? After all, she was going to marry your father."

Blake made a face. "Hardly, we tolerated her for Dad's sake but she was a mean, nasty person."

"Did you guys feel threatened that she was going to steal away the Toliver money?" Lexy asked innocently.

"I know that's what most people think - I'm sure we're high up on the suspect list, but I wasn't worried about it. Dad has trust funds in place for us."

"And Bronson?"

"You'd have to ask him. But I'm not sure he cares too much about money."

"What about Chastine's assistant...what was her name?"

"Candace?"

"Yes, that's it! I didn't catch her last name though..." Lexy said it nonchalantly, as if she didn't really care.

She saw Blake's forehand wrinkle. He paused for a moment. "Come to think of it, I don't think I know her last name."

Damn.

Lexy was about to press further when she was interrupted by the trilling of her phone. She pulled it out of her pocket, glancing down at the display. *Jack!* Why did he have to call now of all times? With a sigh, she turned the phone off without answering and stuffed it back in her pocket.

"Who was that?" Blake asked.

"Oh, no one important." She turned her full attention back to Blake, tilting her head sideways, glancing at him from underneath her long lashes. "So, what were we talking about?"

Out of the corner of her eye, Lexy could see Cassie was finishing up with collecting the trays and other items. She'd have to either give Cassie a signal to slow down or speed up her questioning. She didn't have all her answers yet and wouldn't have an excuse to stay unless she wanted to get *really* friendly with Blake. Which she didn't.

"Enough about the murder...I know a place where we can talk much more comfortably...and about something much more interesting." Blake leaned in closer to Lexy, his boyish good looks and charm were tempting but Lexy had more important things to do.

"Oh, Blake, you're such a flirt!" She laughed, making a joke out of it. "But seriously, aren't you the least bit curious about who could have murdered your future stepmother right in your own home? I mean it's kind of creepy that a murderer was in your house."

"Well, since you put it *that* way...it is kind of troubling."

"You were home, right? Did you hear anything?"

"I *was* home that night. We all were because the brunch was the next day. It's pretty quiet up in the upper wings, but I did hear a commotion early in the morning..." His voice trailed off, his eyes moving up to the ceiling apparently thinking back to the night before the murder.

"What was it?" Lexy prompted, trying not to appear too anxious for the answer.

"I thought I heard a woman giggling, but when I poked my head out into the hall, I only saw Bronson coming up the stairs - alone. I thought maybe he brought some floozy home, but there was no one."

"What time was that? If he was just coming up from downstairs he might have been very close to running into the murderer!" Or maybe he *was* the murderer, Lexy thought.

"It was around 2:30" Blake said, then Lexy saw his eyes grow wider. "Hey, isn't that right about when the murder happened?"

Lexy nodded.

Blake turned his charm on Lexy. "But, what's any of that have to do with us?"

Lexy felt a sharp jolt of panic when he took her arm in an attempt to lead her into the other room.

The sound of trays clattering behind them brought them to a halt. Lexy spun around, feeling a surge of relief when she saw Cassie standing in front of two trays which had fallen on the floor.

"Sorry," Cassie said. Lexy noticed she didn't look the least bit sorry. "I'm all done packing this stuff up, Lexy."

"Oh...right." Lexy looked up at Blake. "We should be getting back to the bakery."

"Oh...but we were just getting to know each other." Lexy thought she saw an actual look of regret on his face, but she knew he was a notorious playboy - he'd probably forget about her as soon as she walked out the door.

The sound of the door knocker echoed into the kitchen. Lexy took advantage of the new visitors to make her exit. "You go answer that - Cassie and I will let ourselves out the back. Our car is just round to the front."

"OK, well maybe I'll see you later?" It was more a question than a statement.

Lexy nodded and they both started off in opposite directions - Blake towards the front door, Lexy towards the back.

Remembering she needed one final piece of information, Lexy stopped and spun around. "Blake?"

"Yes?"

"I was just wondering when the wake is. My grandmother would like to pay her respects."

"Oh, that's set for tomorrow afternoon. Three o'clock at McGreevy's."

"Great, thanks!" Lexy turned back, grabbed one of the boxes Cassie had packed from the table and beat a hasty retreat out the back door.

Chapter Nine

"Not that way, Cassie - this way." Lexy nodded her head towards the back of the house.

"Huh? Our car is that way," Cassie said, pointing towards the front of the house.

"I know, but we're going this way because I have a sneaky suspicion this is where the murder weapon can be found."

"Murder weapon?"

"Yes, remember yesterday when John told us it was the seven inch serrated knife? Well, I think it was one of our knives! I had brought it here during the initial setup and now, it's missing. It's got to be the one the killer used."

For a fleeting second Lexy wondered if the fact that it was their knife would cast suspicion on her - after all she *had* been the one to find the body. She didn't think she would be a suspect though - she had no motive. But it gave her even more of a reason to find the knife which she hoped might have some evidence on or near it that would help them figure out who the killer was.

"OK, so it was our knife, why the trip to the back of the house?" Cassie asked.

"I happened to notice a little dumpster back here behind this fence. Seems like that would be a perfect place to dispose of a murder weapon."

"But do you think we should be looking for it? Maybe we should call the police - I mean we wouldn't want to destroy any evidence or anything."

Cassie wanting to call the police? Now this was a switch, Lexy thought. Usually she avoided any kind of authority.

Cassie did have a good point, though. Lexy had considered calling them but she didn't have time to wait for the police to find it, plus she was still mad at Jack.

The girls slipped behind a stockade fence which camouflaged the unsightly necessities like the dumpster and central air conditioning unit for the house from the view of the mansion. It was also a convenient camouflage for them in case anyone happened to look out one of the windows.

Over to the right, on the other side of the fence was a gigantic pool, sparkling blue water and Grecian statues all around. The construction of a new cabana building - the size of most peoples homes - was in full swing on the other side of the pool.

Lexy tore her eyes from the peaceful scene to look at the grungy, smelly dumpster. Putting down her box, she stepped gingerly over the greasy debris on the ground. Next to her Cassie wrinkled her nose in disgust.

"It smells pretty ripe out here, huh?" Lexy pinched her nose between her thumb and forefinger to block out the smell of garbage. With her other hand she swatted at several flies who were circling her.

"So, who's going to look in there?" Cassie asked.

Lexy looked at her friend, then at the dumpster, then took a deep breath. "I will."

She walked over to the edge and tried to peek in. It was a small dumpster, but even standing on her tippy toes with 2" platforms, she couldn't see over the edge. Glancing around she found a milk crate in the corner, pulled it over and stepped up on top allowing herself a view into the dumpster. She felt bile rise up in her throat, the smell was even worse from up there.

" I don't see it..." Lexy craned her head to look into the corner of the dumpster.

"Of course not, what were you expecting, to have the murder weapon just laying on top? If the murderer has any sense it'll be buried deep down inside there." Cassie blew out a breath causing her pink tinted bangs to flutter.

Lexy looked down into the dumpster again. *Could she bring herself to get in there?* The thought caused her stomach to churn, the Danish she ate earlier threatening to make its way back up.

She looked around for a better solution. Over in the corner was a large push broom - if she used it to stir things around, maybe she could unearth the knife.

"Cassie, grab that broom over there for me."

Cassie grabbed the handle, and passed it over to Lexy. Lexy hoisted herself up, balancing her hips on the edge of the dumpster so she could get the broom down inside. Glancing at Cassie over her shoulder, she asked "Can you hold my legs so I don't fall in?"

Lexy heard Cassie burst out laughing, then felt her grab her right calf.

She shoved the broom in and started sweeping the garbage around which sent a variety of noxious smells up to assault her nose. Her eyes weren't having much fun either - there was all kinds of gross, slimy garbage, flies and who knew what else in there.

"Ughh...this is gross!" She moved the broom slowly, her eyes searching for a glint of silver or the shape of a knife handle. She was just getting into a sweeping routine when-

"What are you doing?" The deep voice boomed from behind them.

Cassie shrieked, throwing her arms in the air, she let go of Lexy's leg. Lexy teetered on the edge of the dumpster - her rear end up in the air, her arms flailing for something to grab onto to save her from falling in.

Just as she was about to lose her battle, she felt someone grab her by the waist and pull her off the side of the dumpster. She let out a sigh of relief, then turned, coming face to face with the person who had saved her from being smothered in garbage. The *last* person she wanted to see right now. *Jack Perillo.*

***

"What were you doing in the dumpster?" Jack demanded.

Lexy felt a surge of anger bubble up inside her when she saw the hint of laughter in his eyes. She tried to back away from him but was forced to stop when her backside bumped up against the hard metal of the dumpster.

"I was looking for some of my catering equipment," she mumbled. Looking down, she swatted at her clothing to try to remove some of the encrusted debris.

She heard Jack sigh. "Lexy, I hope you aren't meddling in this case."

Meddling? What did he think - she had nothing better to do? If he had been doing his job faster, she wouldn't be forced to figure out who the murderer was in order to get the payment in the first place! The anger Lexy had felt earlier threatened to explode. She struggled to remain calm. Her eyes darted to the left. She considered side-stepping away from him but he put his hands against the dumpster on either side of her, trapping her in between them.

"And why haven't you answered my calls?"

Calls? Had he called more than just the one time today? Lexy realized she hadn't checked her messages in a couple of days.

She saw Jack's eyes soften, he reached over, pushing a lock of hair behind her ears. "By the way...you look nice today." Lexy felt her heart clench, the words caught her off-guard, chiseling away at her anger.

Then suddenly, he was leaning in to kiss her. She stood there frozen. *Did she want him to kiss her?* His lips softly brushed against hers causing Lexy to feel delicious tingles in all the right places. She was just about to return the kiss when she remembered how he had been ignoring her the past few weeks. Then her thoughts drifted to his earlier comment about meddling and hard, cold anger chased away those warm and fuzzy tingles.

She pushed on his chest with her hands, shoving him away from her.

"I hope you don't think you can just breeze in here and kiss me after ignoring me for two weeks." She blurted out the words, stabbing her index finger at his chest to punctuate them.

Jack took a step backwards, a look of surprise on his face. Then, before he could say anything, she turned on her heel and stomped off.

Rounding the corner of the fence, Lexy glanced up at the house and saw a curtain flutter back. *Was someone watching her?*

Not looking where she was going, she plowed full force into the back of Cassie, pushing her into John Darling almost causing the three of them to fall down in a tangled pile.

"What the heck-?" Lexy noticed John had caught Cassie in his arms to keep her from knocking him down. Neither one of them looked too upset about it. In fact, it seemed like Cassie took a bit longer extracting herself than necessary.

"Sorry." Lexy looked at Cassie, then nodded her head towards the car. "Let's go." She picked up her box, storming off towards the front of the house.

Lexy put the box in the trunk, then slipped into the driver's seat. She looked at herself in the rear view mirror - her hair was messed up, she had dirt on her face and her eye was twitching like a metronome.

She pulled her phone from her pocket. Jack *had* called yesterday. She dialed her inbox. Her heart flip-flopped when she heard the apologetic message he had left the day before. He really did care. She glanced over in the direction of the dumpster. *Should she go back to talk to him?*

Her thoughts were interrupted by Cassie's appearance from the side of the house. She watched Cassie slide her box into the trunk, then open the passenger door plopping herself into the seat.

"What took you so long?" Lexy asked.

Cassie turned, looking Lexy straight in the face. "Did you ever hear the saying - you catch more flies with honey than vinegar?"

Lexy nodded, thinking about all the flies by the dumpster but not sure where Cassie was going with this.

"Well, while you were busy fighting with Jack, I was talking nicely with John...and I found out something very interesting."

Lexy raised her eyebrows, indicating for Cassie to elaborate.

"Apparently one of the sons, Bronson, has a history of violence. John said the police have picked him up a few times for fighting." Cassie, sat back a proud look on her face.

"That *is* interesting." Lexy tapped her fingernail on her front teeth. "And I bet you won't find any record of it because the Toliver money can come in handy for making stuff like that go away."

Cassie nodded "Yep, John said all those records usually get closed and purged from the public files."

"Which makes me wonder...what other kinds of things Toliver money might have made *go away*?" She glanced nervously back up at the house.

"Good find, though. Nans and the girls will be proud!" She turned back to Cassie and held out her fist for a knuckle tap. "Speaking of which, I better run home to shower and change. They're expecting me at the Retirement Center after lunch."

Chapter Ten

Lexy sailed into the Brooke Ridge Retirement Center refreshed from her recent shower and balancing a box of Danish. She put the box on the table. Opening the lid she waved her hand at it indicating for Nans, Ida, Ruth and Helen to help themselves.

Ruth, Nans and Helen dug in. Lexy pushed the box towards Ida who held her hand up, palm out. "None for me, thanks."

Three pairs of eyes turned towards Ida, the Danish pastries paused midway to their mouths.

"It's that new gentlemen on the third floor, isn't it?" Ruth's said.

Lexy was surprised to see Ida's cheeks turned pink. "No, I'm just gaining a little weight is all," she stammered eliciting a giggle from the other women.

"OK, let's get down to business." Nans voice boomed over the giggling. She turned to Lexy. "Were you able to find anything out?"

"Cassie and I went back to the Tolivers and I talked to Blake. Both the sons were home that night but I found out something else. Xavier's ex-girlfriend has appeared back on the scene."

"Oh, that's right," Nans said, "he was dating that actress, Trixie...what was her last name?" She asked turning to Helen her eyebrows raised in a question.

Helen punched the button on her iPad bringing it to life on the table in front of her. "Should be easy enough to find out, they were all over the society pages a few years back." She punched in a few keys then sat back with a satisfied smile. "Yep, here it is - Trixie Masters."

"Yes, that's it! We'll need to do some checking up on her - I wonder where *she* was when Chastine was killed?"

"Speaking of which, did either one of the Toliver boys have an alibi?" Ruth asked around a mouthful of cherry Danish.

"They were both home but, both were alone." Lexy peered into the box of Danish, choosing one with a gooey apple center. "Blake said he saw Bronson out in the hallway around 2:30 that morning. He also said he thought he heard a woman giggling but he didn't see anyone."

"And what about the murder weapon?"

Lexy felt her stomach clench. "Umm...it turns out the murder weapon is actually one of the knives I brought there...and it seems to be missing."

"Oh, well maybe we should be investigating you, then." Ida joked.

"Very funny," Lexy said. Picking up her Danish, she took a dainty bite from the edge. "I don't think the police know it was my knife yet. I was hoping to find it today when I looked around out by the dumpster."

"What did *you* guys find out?" She asked, taking another bite from the edge of the Danish.

"Ruth did some research on Chastine. We found an article about her being engaged to some oil tycoon down in Texas, but apparently it didn't work out and she moved out here."

"We couldn't find too much about the Toliver boys. Bronson was discharged from the military and there seems to be some controversy over that. Blake is a bit of a playboy - you probably already knew that," Nans looked at Lexy over the tops of her glasses as she read from their notes. "Of course, Chastine would have gotten control of the bulk of the Toliver money after she married Xavier so both boys would have had a motive to kill her."

Lexy considered the information while she ate her way around the edge of her Danish, carefully saving the middle for last. She didn't think Blake had anything to do with the murder, but Bronson's military discharge added an interesting element.

"According to the police, Bronson has been picked up a few times for fighting. I wonder if his military discharge has anything to do with being violent?"

Lexy saw Helen's brows wrinkle together. "We didn't find any police record for Bronson."

"Yeah, apparently all the records were sealed, or whatever they do to them to get them out of public view. That's what money can do for you, I guess."

"Speaking of money...the ex-girlfriend, Trixie must have been upset about getting dumped - I wonder if getting back with Xavier, and his money, would be motive enough for murder?" Ida asked.

Lexy savored the last few bites of the outside edge of her Danish while she watched Helen's fingers tap quickly on the iPad. Helen gave a final, exaggerated tap then nodded with approval spinning the tablet around so everyone could see the screen. "It looks like Trixie does have some priors." Helen said, pointing her finger at the screen.

Priors? Lexy smiled to herself. The police jargon seemed odd coming from a 70-ish year old woman, but then again so did the fact that she was using an iPad to investigate murder suspects.

Lexy craned her neck over the table to get a better look at the information displayed on the tablet's screen. It reminded her of the police blotter listing. "That looks official, how did you find it?"

Helen shrugged sheepishly. "I'm not supposed to tell, but your friend Jack gave us special access to the police database, seeing as we help them so much and all."

Jack had given them special access? Great. He'd probably been spending more time with the Ladies Detective Club lately than he had with her. Her stomach flip flopped at the thought of him. She remembered the message he had left, apologizing for being so busy lately. She made a mental note to call him back as soon as she was done. After all, he had made the first move and she should at least give him another chance.

Nans's voice brought her attention back to the iPad. "These all look like minor things - fights with other women and complaints. But if the stakes were high, including millions of dollars, maybe Trixie would see her way to something more fatal than just a cat fight."

"But she wasn't in the house that night so she might have had a motive but not the opportunity." Ruth chimed in.

"Well, actually she might have. Blake told me the back door to the kitchen was open, so it looks like anyone could have come in the house through that door, murdered Chastine, and slipped out again." Lexy popped the gooey apple covered center of the Danish in her mouth.

"Well, there are so many suspects, this is going to be an interesting one to unravel." Nans said, her eyes bright with the challenge. "We do have our feelers out about that pin you said was missing from Chastine's blouse. If someone pawns it, we'll know."

"I bet we'll learn a lot at the wake," Ida said excitedly. "On TV that's where they find out the best information." The other ladies nodded their agreement.

Lexy let out a sigh. She hated going to wakes, but when her ex had been murdered earlier in the summer, the ladies had insisted she go to his. They had been right. She *had* learned quite a bit at the wake. "Blake said it is scheduled for tomorrow at 3:00."

"Great! You can pick us up here at 2:30 - we'll all go together!" Nans said excitedly with Ruth, Ida and Helen nodding in agreement.

Lexy's mind conjured up an image of the four women skulking around the wake in tan London Fog raincoats taking notes on their iPads. She could hardly wait.

Chapter Eleven

Lexy sat in her car in the retirement center parking lot thinking about the messages Jack had left on her phone. The mid-fall sun beat through her windshield raising the temperature in the car to summer like levels. The Danish she had polished off inside, suddenly felt like a lead weight in her stomach.

She stared at the cell phone in her hand. She *wanted* to call Jack but the thought of talking to him sent her stomach in a tailspin. She did want to clear the air and work things out with him, but she had to admit she had an ulterior motive for calling. She wanted to know if they found the murder weapon in the dumpster. She realized she should probably come clean about the missing knife, she didn't want it to reflect badly on her if Jack found out she had withheld that little tidbit of information. She took a deep breath, then pressed the call button.

"Perillo." She heard Jack's voice bark his customary greeting.

"Hi Jack...it's Lexy," she said tentatively, not sure what, exactly, to expect.

"Oh, Lexy. I was hoping you would call." Lexy's heart did a flip-flop upon hearing the tenderness in his voice when he said her name.

"Look, I want to apologize. I guess I've been neglecting you. I didn't mean to...it's just that I've been so busy on this other case I am on. I tend to get wrapped up in my work." Jack sounded nervous which made Lexy's heart melt, washing away the past two weeks of anger and hurt feelings. She realized how silly she had been to think he had lost interest in her. He just got busy with work. How insecure could she be?

"Well, I *was* feeling a bit neglected," she laughed, "I didn't know if you were trying to give me the brush off."

"No, its nothing like that. You know how I feel about you." *She did?* Come to think of it, Jack had never *said* how he felt about her, but he did act like he cared. And he sure sounded like it on the phone right now. Lexy decided to let go of her insecurities and accept that things were good with them.

Having that out of the way, she turned to more pressing issues. "Were you looking for something in the dumpster, today?" She asked, trying to slip the words in as if they were just conversational.

"Were you?"

"I asked first."

Jack's deep laugh warmed her from the other side of the phone. "Okay, I give. We were looking for the murder weapon - it still hasn't shown up. Now it's your turn, what we you looking for?"

Lexy crossed her fingers. "I was looking for some of our supplies which seem to have disappeared from the house." She hoped her voice didn't reveal the little white lie, but she didn't want Jack to know she was looking for the murder weapon because she knew he would be mad at her for "meddling".

"Oh really? Like one of your knives maybe?"

Damn, he already knows the murder weapon was my knife.

"Well, now that you mention it, I am missing some knives," she said innocently.

"Lexy, I wasn't born yesterday. I know you were looking for the murder weapon in there *and* I know it was one of your knives. What I don't know is why you would be trying to find it yourself instead of leaving it up to the police."

Lexy didn't have a good answer, other than the police were being to slow in finding the murderer. She chose to remain silent.

She heard the rustle of papers from Jack's end, then he said, "I have to run, but maybe we can talk about this later...say over dinner Thursday night?"

"OK." Lexy didn't know if she should be happy at the prospect of having dinner with Jack or nervous because he wanted to talk more about the murder weapon.

" Good. I'll pick you up around seven - oh, and Lexy?"

"Yes..."

"I really mean it about staying out of the case. There is a killer on the loose and you could be in danger. I don't want anything to happen to you. Will you promise me that you'll stop your investigation?"

"What?... you're breaking up I can't hear you..." Lexy grabbed an empty candy bar wrapper which was laying on the console and made crinkling noises with it near the phone. "I'll see you Thursday night," she said into the phone, then snapped it shut.

***

Jack held the phone away from his ear looking at it with amusement. He knew Lexy had manufactured the cell phone disturbance to avoid the question. He had to admit he thought it was kind of cute...and funny. He thought lots of things that Lexy did were cute and funny - thats what he liked about her. *Really* liked.

Thinking about her made his heart do a summersault - he hoped she would take his warning seriously. According to what the investigation was revealing, they could be dealing with a very dangerous and unstable person. He didn't want Lexy to put herself into danger by continuing to investigate on her own.

Jack leaned back in his chair. He was surprised at the way his stomach knotted up when he thought about harm coming to Lexy. She'd become very important to him over these past few months. He had real feelings for her, feelings he didn't think he would ever have again after his breakup with Caitlin.

The breakup with his former fiancee had been hard on him, mostly because Jack blamed himself for always putting his job first and neglecting her. The same thing he had been doing the past two weeks with Lexy. A deep feeling of dread washed over him at the thought of losing Lexy. He couldn't let that happen. He would have to make a conscious effort to pay more attention to her. Hopefully it wasn't already too late.

"It looks like our suspicions were right about the Toliver boys." Jack jerked his head up, startled by his partner, John Darling, who had suddenly appeared beside his desk.

"They're both flat broke and living off Daddy's money," John continued, handing a stack of papers to Jack. "Not only *that* but I'm digging up some really creepy stuff from their high school days. You remember the murder of that young girl back about twenty years ago?" Jack nodded. "Well, it seems like either Blake or Bronson or maybe both of them may have been mixed up in it."

Jack rubbed his face with his hands. He didn't like the idea of a dangerous murderer on the loose in his town but he didn't have anything concrete on either of the boys to bring them in and hold them on. He wasn't sure that one of them actually *was* the murderer and there was a long list of other suspects to eliminate first.

"We have to think about who had the opportunity. It had to have been someone in the house, or someone who had access. We know the front door was open that morning and the back door was too - but who opened them and why?" Jack asked.

John spread his hands. "There's a lot of questions waiting to be answered. Why did Chastine leave Texas so abruptly? Why can't we find anything about her assistant, Candice? Who left the doors open?"

Jack looked up at him. "The biggest question I have is...why was Chastine down in the kitchen all dressed up in fancy clothes at two thirty in the morning when she should have been in bed sleeping? That would seem to indicate she was meeting someone. I think if we find out who that someone was, we may have our killer."

Chapter Twelve

Lexy breathed a sigh of relief that Nans and the girls weren't wearing trench coats like she had imagined. They were quite tastefully dressed complete with fresh hair-do's and toting their gigantic purses. Lexy wondered if their iPads inside them.

Lexy jumped out of the car, pushing up the front seats so the ladies could have access to the back. She eyed the tiny space in her VW beetle uncertainly. *Could three elderly women contort themselves into this space?*

"This is pretty cramped, are you guys going to be able to get in here?" She voiced her concern.

"Oh don't be silly," Ruth waived her hand, "we do yoga, this is a piece of cake." To prove the point Ruth, Ida and Helen all piled into the back seat with the ease of gymnasts.

Nans took the passenger seat and Lexy hopped back into the driver seat, putting the car in gear and heading off towards the funeral parlor.

She pulled up in front of McGreevy's, dropping the ladies off at the door, marveling at how easily they extracted themselves from the back seat.

Lexy drove around back to the parking area. Getting out of the car, she inspected her black skirt for any spots of flour, twisting around to look at the back. She'd been so busy at the bakery, she barely had time to do a quick change and fluff up her hair before driving over to pick the ladies up. Once she was satisfied that her skirt was flour-free, she straightened her peach colored silk blouse and strode off towards the front.

The ladies were waiting for her on the steps. Ida looked her up and down, stopping at her black suede Stuart Weitzman four inch pumps. The contrasting silver metallic pointed toe added a touch of glam to the understated shoe.

"I used to be able to wear heels like that," Ida said wistfully. Then she leaned in towards Lexy and whispered, "You shouldn't wear them too often though, dear, or you'll end up with bunions like mine."

Lexy looked down at Ida's feet. They were clad in low-slung sandals. The open toe style, which Lexy thought was a little late for this time of year, afforded a perfect view of Ida's big toe which was contorted over to the side, bunching up her other toes. It looked painful. Lexy shuddered looking back down at her own feet. Maybe she should rethink her choice of footwear from now on.

The ladies hurried up to the oak doors which were opened, as if by magic, by two somber looking gentlemen in dark suits.

Lexy followed them inside. The funeral home was exactly as she remembered it from Kevin's wake. It was elegantly decorated and exuded the faint scent of flowers. The hushed tones of low voices and hymnal music filled her ears.

They had the casket setup in the room to the right. Nans and the others made a beeline in that direction. Lexy almost had to jog to keep up. She got in line behind them, dutifully waiting her turn to file past the body on her way to pay her respects to the family.

On the other side, Xavier, Blake and Bronson were standing in a receiving line. Lexy was surprised to see a blonde woman hovering around Xavier alternating between handing him tissues and shoving a small glass of water in his hand. Lexy poked Nans in the ribs. "Who's that?" she whispered indicating the blonde.

"That's his ex., Trixie. I guess she didn't waste any time trying to get her hooks back into him."

Lexy watched her from her spot in line. She seemed generally concerned about Xavier, almost motherly. Could she have killed Chastine? She didn't look like a hard-boiled killer, but, then Lexy didn't really know what one was supposed to look like.

Lexy shuffled up to the casket behind Nans, Ruth,Ida and Helen. The four of them stood together, looking down at Chastine.

"She *was* really beautiful." Ruth said. The rest of them murmured their agreement. Lexy remembered the few times she had met her in person. She *had* been a true beauty. No wonder she was able to charm Xavier into marrying her.

Nans turned to the receiving line. She went straight to Xavier giving her old friend a hug and telling him how sorry she was. Trixie flitted around in the background keeping a respectful distance but staying at the ready whenever Xavier seemed to need a pat on the back or a fresh tissue.

Lexy followed behind Nans, giving her condolences to Xavier, then Bronson. She was surprised to find Bronson was rather civil - nice even. But he was behaving rather nervously, his eyes darting around the room as if he was looking for someone.

Blake was at the end of the line. He spent a little more time than necessary hugging Lexy in an attempt to grope certain parts of her. The man was shameless! She offered her condolences and he shrugged it off opting to ask her out on a date instead. Lexy extracted herself from his clutches by promising to catch up with him later, then escaped from the receiving line as fast as she could.

She regrouped with Nans and the girls in a small room off to the side.

"I say we split up and canvas the room to see if we can find anything out," Nans whispered.

The others nodded, then everyone took off in a different direction. Lexy headed straight for the side room where they usually kept the refreshments.

The room was long and narrow. It was set up much the same as it had been for Kevin's wake with a long table against the wall loaded with trays of cookies and pastry. She wondered what bakery they came from. Grabbing a lemon cookie, she gingerly took a bite. They weren't nearly as good as hers -

maybe she should bring the funeral director some samples.

Lexy drifted over to the corner of the room, the lemon cookie balanced in one hand on top of a napkin. Voices drifted towards her, allowing her to pick up snippets of conversations.

"....loved her so much."

"She was a real ..."

"I could have killed her myself..."

Lexy's ears perked up when she heard that last bit. She honed in on the conversation like a guided missile. Three people she didn't recognize were huddled together in the corner just outside the snack room. Lexy slipped out of the room, and edged along the wall, sidestepping a little closer. There was a tall potted plant between her and the three people and she used it for cover, standing behind it, but with her ear cocked towards the threesome.

"Y'all knew I had to come just to make sure that beetch was dead." It was a woman with a heavy southern accent.

"That's raat, after what she did to Bob, we owed it to him to fly up." Another southern accent - this one a man.

"I couldda spet on her, but t'wouldn't be gentlemanly."

The voices got softer. Lexy couldn't hear what they were saying so she leaned closer. She was practically in the tree but leaned in even closer still. A jolt of horror shot through her when she realized she had gone too far. The giant plant was tipping over!

She dropped her cookie on the floor. Her hands grabbed at the plant, trying to keep it from falling but managing only to pull off a handful of leaves. She felt her stomach sinking as she watched the plant descending towards the group. Luckily one of the men had quick reactions. He jumped up blocking the plant from falling and setting it upright again.

"Well, little lady, I guess maybe you should be looking where you're going." The man said with a friendly wink.

Lexy felt her cheeks grow hot. "I'm so sorry," she stammered.

The man let out a chuckle and stuck his hand out towards her. "I'm Dinty Carter, and this here is my wife Mandy and my brother Harold." He pointed to the other two people who were with him.

Lexy put her hand out. His handshake was firm and warm. "Lexy Baker." She introduced herself. "You don't sound like you're from around here, were you friends of Chastine's from back home?"

Mandy let out a snicker, "Haadly, that woman dint have any friends."

Lexy raised her eyebrows. "You didn't like her but you came all the way here from..." She let her voice trail off, she didn't actually know where they were from.

"Texas." Dinty filled in. "Chastine was engaged to our good friend Bob, and ... well... she did a numbah on him. Poor man's not been the same since she left him - almost catatonic. Won't talk to anyone, even his own daughter. We felt like we owed it ta him ta come up and see for ourselves - maybe he can git some closure and start ta heal."

"Cripes what did she *do* to him?" Lexy asked.

Dinty spread his hands and shrugged his wide shoulders. "Lied, cheated and broke his heart."

Lexy felt sympathy for the man. She looked over into the other room where Chastine lay. Clearly these people must have hated her to make the trip all the way up here - but did they hate her enough to kill her?

***

Lexy spent the next half-hour rambling around the funeral parlor listening covertly to peoples conversations. She talked with a few people she knew from town, but no one had any light to shed on the murder. She was starting to feel conspicuous when Nans found her and announced it was time to go.

They were making their way down the large front steps when Lexy heard a familiar voice behind her.

"There's my favorite girl!" She whirled around to see Jack, her heart swelling. She beamed a wide smile at him, but, instead of rushing over to Lexy, Jack made a beeline straight for Nans. She felt her smile dim just a bit. Encircling the older woman in a hug, Jack winked pointedly at Lexy.

"Mona, how have you been?" Jack asked.

"Wonderful! How about you?" Mona stood on her tip toes, giving Jack a peck on the cheek.

Lexy felt her cheeks grow warm, embarrassed at her momentary misplaced jealousy. Jack lived in the house behind Lexy - the house Nans had lived in for decades. During the last few years, Nans and Jack had become rather close with Jack doing odd jobs around the house to help her out. Lexy knew Jack admired the spunky old lady and he got a kick out of the Ladies Detective Club. He often tried to help them out by feeding them clues and giving them tips. Nans thought of Jack almost like a grandson, it was no surprise she was his "favorite girl".

Jack let go of Nans. Moving over next to Lexy, he put his arm around her. "What are you ladies doing here?" He asked, his eyes narrowing at Lexy.

"Nans and the girls wanted to pay their respects to Xavier - they've been friends since childhood. I just gave her a ride." Lexy looked at him sideways from under her lashes, her face a mask of innocence.

Jack gave her a look indicating his skepticism.

"Well, I hope you guys don't get too involved in this case," He said to Nans and the other women. "The killer could be very dangerous. I don't want anything to happen to my favorite girls." He glanced over at Lexy, his face as hard as stone.

"I better be getting inside...Lexy, I'll see you tomorrow?"

Lexy nodded enthusiastically feeling a warm tingle start in her lower stomach at the thought of seeing Jack for dinner.

Jack nodded, then turned and walked up the steps to the front doors.

"Such a nice young man," Ruth said.

"And handsome too," Ida added as she watched him walk away.

The women started walking back towards Lexy's car. "So, did anyone find out anything good?" Lexy asked.

"I happened to run into Mavis Fencer - she said Chastine had a lover." Ruth's eyes were wide, her voice barely above a whisper.

"Interesting..." Lexy chewed her bottom lip. "Maybe the lover was upset she was getting married and killed her - or maybe Xavier found out and killed her in a fit of passion!"

"I heard a few younger people talking about Bronson's temper, apparently he can be violent when he gets mad. Maybe Chastine made him mad that morning and he did her in?" Helen said, then turning to Lexy, "Did you find anything out?"

"As a matter of fact, I did." She told them about the Texans, omitting the part about her knocking over the tree.

"Do you think they could have done it?" Helen asked.

"They said they were only here for the wake - to get closure for their friend."

"I think we should find out how long they *have* been here. If what they say is true, then they can't have been here more than a day. Maybe you can check the local hotels to see when they checked in." She said to Ruth then, looking at the group, she added, "If they were here *before* she died then their story is a bit fishy."

"They *could* have come here from Texas to kill her...anyone could have - to avenge this Bob person." Lexy thought for a moment. "Actually they said Bob had a daughter - she might have hated Chastine enough to want to kill her after what she did to her father."

"We need to check into this daughter, find out who she is and, more importantly, *where* she was when Chastine was murdered," Nans said. "Also, we need to find out who Chastine's secret lover was."

Lexy ushered the women into the car and got behind the wheel. She felt a sinking sensation in her stomach. They were no closer to solving the murder than they had been that morning. Quite the opposite, in fact, they had come to the wake hoping to narrow things down and had ended up with even more suspects than when they started!

Chapter Thirteen

Lexy sat at the counter in the back of the bakery sorting through the mountain of mail which had accumulated over the past few days. When she got to an envelope with red edges, she felt her heart freeze. It was from the appliance vendor. She ripped it open letting the envelope drift to the floor.

It was due in seven days!

Lexy looked around the kitchen, she couldn't risk having that payment held up by the Toliver murder any longer. She needed to get down to business and catch Chastine's killer. The only problem was, she still had no idea who might have done it.

She reached into a drawer, pulling out a pen and paper. Mentally running through the list of suspects, she tried to figure out who would be most likely. The people from Texas were a long shot, although, if Bob's daughter could be found, and she was here at the time of the murder, she would be a likely candidate.

She wrote Bob's daughter down on the paper with an asterisk next to it. Then below it wrote Dinty Carter with a dash next to his name.

Lexy had her doubts about Xavier discovering Chastine had a lover and killing her over it - he seemed genuinely upset about her death. She wrote his name down on the paper and lightly crossed it out.

Chastine's lover was another suspect. Lexy wondered if she actually did have one or if it was just a rumor. It seemed foolish for the woman to jeopardize her upcoming marriage by cheating on Xavier, but Lexy added "Chastine's lover" to the list just in case.

Trixie could have done it. She certainly was taking advantage of Chastine's death to rekindle her relationship with Xavier. The incentive of marrying into all that money could easily justify murder in some peoples eyes. Lexy wrote Trixie's name down on the list under Xavier's and put an asterisk next to it.

Finally, her thoughts turned to Bronson and Blake. Either one of them *could* have done it. They had means, motive and opportunity so she added their names at the bottom.

She studied the list. Seven suspects. They all had a motive. She figured she could narrow down the list by crossing off the ones who had an alibi for the time of the murder.

Of course, she had no idea who two of the suspects even were, which could make it a little difficult. Maybe she should focus on the ones she *did* know. The question was which one to focus on first.

Her thoughts were interrupted by the trilling of her phone. It was Nans.

"Hi, Nans," Lexy chirped into the phone.

"Morning!" The older woman bubbled. "We have some information about some of the suspects. I wanted to let you know right away."

Lexy felt her heart grow lighter - she was already making progress!

"Ruth checked with the local hotels. Your friend Dinty Carter and his posse from Texas, arrived only yesterday. She also found out they flew in on a private jet - apparently Dinty has some money. But since the jet only flew in yesterday they couldn't have murdered Chastine."

"Great!" Lexy gingerly crossed Dinty Carter's name off the list.

"And there's more," Nans continued. "Trixie couldn't have murdered her either because she was seen at an after party by hundreds of people. Her picture was even in the paper."

"An after party?"

"Yes, Trixie is an actress in the theater downtown - she plays a small role in their rendition of *A Midsummer Nights Dream*, which just opened this weekend. It's common for them to have a party after the play, which tends to go on until all hours of the night. Ida knows the director and some of the other people in the play - she checked with them - Trixie was there, enjoying herself fully, at two-thirty in the morning."

Lexy felt overjoyed - two down and only five to go! She crossed Trixie's name off the list.

"Thanks a bunch Nans, this really narrows down my suspect list. Now I've only got to whittle it down to just one person - the killer."

"We did find out one other thing which might help you with that. Helen sent a description of the brooch you said Chastine usually wears - the one you think was ripped from her blouse - out to the local pawn shops and we got a bite. *AtoZ Pawn* over on Chestnut Street said a man brought a brooch in which sounded similar to what you described. It didn't have a big stone in it though, all the stones had been removed. The man wanted to sell it for the melt value of the gold.

"Did he describe what the man looked like?" Lexy felt her heartbeat speed up.

"Helen tried to pump him for information but all he could remember was that the man was tall, dark and seemed like he was in a bad mood. He also said the man was in a hurry which made him a little suspicious, so he didn't take brooch."

Tall, dark and in a bad mood? That sounded a lot like Bronson. Suddenly Lexy knew exactly who to start focusing on first.

***

Lexy raced out to the front of the store. "Cassie!"

Cassie, who was halfway in the display case straightening out a tower of eclairs turned, looking at Lexy over her shoulder with raised eyebrows.

"Want to go for a ride?" She asked, keys dangling from her fingers.

Cassie straightened up. "What? Why?"

"Come on, it's the slow part of the day. Haley can watch the bakery for the rest of the afternoon and then lock up - we have a murderer to catch."

Lexy saw Cassie's brows scrunch together, her sideways glare begged for an explanation.

"I've narrowed down the suspect list to a few people. I was hoping we could do some covert surveillance on them to see what turns up."

Cassie shrugged. "That doesn't seem like something we should be getting ourselves into, does it?"

Lexy felt confused. *Since when did Cassie not want to do something dangerous and, possibly stupid that might get them into trouble with the police?*

She walked over to Cassie putting the back of her hand on her friends forehead in an exaggerated manner. "Are you feeling okay? It'll be an adventure - you're always up for an adventure."

Cassie laughed. "Yeah, I guess so, I don't know what came over me. Let me just finish up this case and I'll grab my jacket."

"Great, we have to swing by my house to pickup Sprinkles first. I'll explain more in the car."

***

Twenty minutes later the girls were loaded into the car with Sprinkles balancing contentedly on the console in between them. Lexy absently patted the dog's silky fur while she told Cassie what she had learned from Nans.

"But, what do you think you will find out from following Bronson?"

"I'm just hoping we'll get lucky. Maybe today will be the day he tries to dispose of the murder weapon. It still hasn't been found, you know." She glanced sideways at her friend. "I got the bill for the kitchen equipment today - it's due in seven days. I'm kind of in a hurry to help get this case closed up."

Lexy felt Cassie put her hand reassuringly on her arm. "Don't worry Lexy, even if you don't get the payment we'll work something out. You will eventually get paid for this job."

"I know, but I don't want to be delinquent on that bill - it could cause a whole lot of problems for us."

The girls fell silent as they got closer to the Toliver mansion. Lexy let off the gas, driving past the house slowly. The Toliver mansion sat next to a nature preserve with walking trials. Lexy pulled her car into the small parking lot for the preserve. She grabbed a pair of binoculars from the backseat.

"It's such a beautiful Indian summer day, I was thinking we could go for a walk in the woods - you know, under the guise of walking the dog, and doing some bird watching with these binoculars. No one needs to know the birds we are watching are the ones in the Toliver house."

Lexy snapped on Sprinkles's dog leash. Jumping out of the car, she left the door open for the little dog to follow. Cassie was already out. Removing her jacket, she tossed it in the back seat.

"It's so warm out, almost like summer!" She stretched turning her face up to the sun.

Sprinkles tugged at the leash, eager to explore. The girls followed her lead, heading down the path.

They walked in silence, enjoying the sounds of the birds, the earthy smell of the woods and the sounds of dry leaves crunching under their feet. They stopped to let Sprinkles explore and sniff along the way. Every so often, they got out the binoculars and trained them on the Toliver house.

The path was close to the Toliver property. Now that the leaves had mostly fallen from the trees, Lexy didn't need binoculars to see into the yard, but she used them to look at the house itself and the various out buildings to try to pick out anything unusual.

After twenty minutes, Lexy sighed with frustration. "There's nothing going on...we should head back."

The path had wound around to the back of the house. They turned to head back towards the car. About halfway back, Lexy noticed the path cut in right near the edge of the Toliver property, where they were building the new cabana. Lexy paused, looking at the construction site through the trees. She was so close, she didn't need binoculars to see they were setting up forms to pour cement.

She felt Sprinkles tugging on the leash. Looking down, she noticed it was wrapped around various sticks and vines, leaving the dog only about a foot of leeway. Lexy squatted down. "How did you do that, girl?" She was always amazed at how the dog could get her leash tangled in an impossible mess. This time was no different - somehow Sprinkles had weaved the leash in and around a cluster of thick vines. Lexy swore under her breath as she tried to unknot the mess.

"Hey, there's a truck idling out front with someone in the passenger seat!" Cassie, who had continued up the path, was now rounding the corner which had a view of the front of the house.

Lexy worked harder at the leash.

"It's Bronson - he's getting in the truck!" Cassie started jogging for the car.

Lexy felt panic rise up in her chest. They had to follow him! Giving up on the leash, she unhooked Sprinkles's harness, scooped the dog up in her arms and ran for the car.

Chapter Fourteen

Lexy peeled out of the parking lot, leaving a cloud of dirt in her wake. Bronson had a good head start, but the road didn't have many intersections so Lexy figured she could catch up to him if she drove fast enough.

"I wonder where he is going...and who is with him?" Cassie rolled down the window, the crisp air circling through the car.

"That's him up ahead!"

They had come to a long straightaway, the taillights of a big black pickup truck signaling to take a right turn were barely visible about a half mile ahead. Lexy stepped on the gas, praying the police had already met their speeding ticket quota for the month.

She lucked out and the light was green when she got to the intersection. She turned right and saw Bronson's truck about 3 cars ahead.

They followed him straight down the road, taking a left when he did but being careful to stay a few cars behind. Lexy was surprised when he pulled into the upscale condo unit on the edge of town.

"I wonder what he would want here?"

"Don't follow directly behind him - it's too obvious," Cassie said. "Go down this side road. We can keep an eye on where his truck is going by watching between the buildings.

They didn't have to go far. Bronson stopped about a half mile in. Lexy did the same. She held her breath as she watched his passenger door opened.

"That's Candice!" She said excitedly.

The girls watched through Cassie's open window as Candice produced a set of keys from her purse than disappeared from view, presumably making her way to the front door of one of the condos.

"She must live here..." Lexy said staring at the back of the condo unit which Candice had just entered. She noticed a big black cat skulking around in the grass between the two buildings. Unfortunately, Sprinkles must have noticed it too. In a blur of white fur, the little dog launched herself out Cassie's open window, charging full speed after the cat. Lexy jumped out of the car in pursuit.

"Sprinkles, come back!" Lexy felt a jolt of panic when she saw the dog disappear around a corner. She tried to run even faster, her stilettos sinking into the soft ground slowed her down and it took a few seconds before she made it around the corner. Her heart sank - the dog was nowhere to be seen!

Then she heard Sprinkles give a playful bark. She turned towards the sound and saw Sprinkles inside one of the condos. The sliding glass door was opened and Sprinkles must have run in. A woman sat on the couch, her head bent down as she petted the dog.

Lexy stepped partway into the condo. "Sprinkles, you almost gave me a heart attack." She gasped between breaths. Sprinkles saw her and ran over, Lexy bent down scooping the dog up into her arms, her cheeks growing warm with embarrassment for the dogs behavior.

"I'm so sorry..." She started to say, then her breath caught in her throat as the woman looked up and she saw who it was. Candice.

***

The two women stared at each other for a few seconds.

"Hey, you're that nosy baker. What are you doing here?"

Nosy baker?

"Umm...my dog got away." Lexy pointed to Sprinkles.

"Yeah but what were you *doing* here in the first place? Were you spying on me?" Candice stood, taking a step forward, her eyes narrowed to slits. Lexy felt her heart clutch in fear.

"No, we were taking Sprinkles," she said, pointing to the dog again, "for a walk and then went for a drive and ended up here." That was mostly true, Lexy thought, mentally crossing her fingers. Candice did not look convinced.

Lexy glanced around the living room of the small condo. It was full of boxes and clutter. "Are you moving?"

Candice snorted, crossing her arms over her chest. "Of course I am, my employer was murdered so now I have no job. So, if you don't mind leaving, I'll get back to packing."

She spat the words out with such hatred that Lexy, backed up a step and stumbled against one of the boxes. It teetered over, the shoes inside threatening to spill out. Lexy put her hand out to stop the box from falling and couldn't help but take a peek at the shoes. She noticed one pair on the top, a gorgeous purple suede with pointy toes. Too bad one of the toes was ruined with a brownish stain. The stain was just on the tip of the toe and extended underneath on the bottom of the shoe where the tan sole showed the true color - red. Red like blood.

Lexy felt a chill trickle up her spine. She clutched Sprinkles closer, putting her finger on her eye to keep it from twitching.

"Why are you still here?" Candice asked, waving her hands at Lexy to shoo her out the door.

Something on Candice's hand caught Lexy's eye. It was a large shiny ring, a ring with a canary yellow cushion cut diamond - just like the one in Chastine's brooch. Lexy backed out the door without a word and bolted for the car.

***

"I...think...Candice is...the killer!" Lexy could barely get the words out between gasps.

Cassie's eyebrows shot up. "What happened out there?"

Lexy took a few deep breaths. "I ran into Candice - Sprinkles was in her condo! She's packing to move."

"That hardly makes her a killer."

"That's not it." Lexy took another deep breath. "While I was there, I noticed some shoes with blood on the tip *and* she had a ring on which had the same stones as the brooch that was missing from Chastine's blouse!

"Wow, that does sound convincing. Should we call the police?"

Lexy grabbed her purse out of the back seat and rummaged in it for her phone, than punched the speed dial number for Jack. She felt her breathing going back to normal as she listened to it ring...and ring...and ring. She snapped the phone shut when it went to his voice mail.

"No answer."

Cassie whipped out her phone. "Let me see if I can get them." Lexy watched her punch in a few numbers then put the phone up to her ear.

"Hi John...good...no, actually I'm calling because Lexy seems to have uncovered the murderer of Chastine Johnson. Yes, she has evidence. OK, see you in a bit."

"Who was that?"

"John Darling. He said to come in right away so they could take a statement." She turned to Lexy, an innocent look on her face. "You're not the only one with an *in* at the police department."

Chapter Fifteen

"Lexy, what are you doing here?" Lexy saw the look of surprise on Jack's face as his eyes traveled from her to Sprinkles to Cassie.

"You didn't talk to John?"

"I didn't catch up with him yet." John's voice boomed from down the hall.

Jack spread his hands "What's this all about?"

"I know who killed Chastine!" Lexy blurted out.

She saw Jack's eyes narrow. "What? I thought I told you to stop investigating the murder?"

Lexy felt her cheeks burn. "I was...well I mean, we were just taking Sprinkles for a walk when we saw Bronson. We followed him and ended up at Candice's condo."

"Lexy, you aren't making sense. Come on down here and tell me the story from the beginning."

Jack turned down the hall and Lexy started to follow. Cassie touched her arm, "I'll stay back here," she said tilting her head in John's direction. Lexy nodded, thinking Cassie probably mistook her eye twitch for a wink. She put her finger up to her eye, wondering if she had a big mascara smudge underneath from jabbing at it to stop the twitch.

Jack stood in front of the door to a plain room motioning for her to enter. Inside was a long table with two metal chairs - one on either side of the table. It looked like the interrogation rooms she always saw on TV. She took a seat, setting Sprinkles down on the floor.

Jack leaned on the edge of the table in front of her and swiped at her cheek gently with his finger. "You had a smudge of mascara there...now, tell me what this is all about."

"Sprinkles got away from me, chasing after a cat. I followed her and, just by chance, she happened to have run into Candice's condo. I went in to get Sprinkles and noticed she had a pair of shoe with blood on the tips." Lexy saw the look of disbelief on Jack's face - she had to admit it did sound a little far fetched.

"What were you doing near Candice's condo...and how do you know it was blood?"

Lexy felt her heart speed up. *How would she explain what she was doing there without getting Jack mad at her?*

"Well..." Lexy saw Jack's eyebrows raising even higher and decided the best course of action was to come clean.

"OK, we followed Bronson. But we weren't going to do anything, just see what he was up to. Only, Sprinkles got out and ran off so I chased after her.

The part about finding Candice in her condo really *did* happen by accident." Lexy looked up at him sheepishly, her heart leaping when she saw amusement, instead of anger, in his eyes.

"What about the blood?"

Lexy told him about the box of shoes. Jack's expression changed as she described exactly what the blood looked like. He took out his notebook and started jotting things down.

"Well, that does sound like blood, but, of course it could be plenty of other things, she could have stepped in it anywhere. I'm afraid it's really not much to go on."

"There is one other thing..." Lexy looked up to see how interested he was in hearing it. Jack bent in closer. "I noticed she had on a ring... a ring with a very distinctive stone in it..."

"A canary yellow cushion cut diamond." Jack finished the sentence for her.

Lexy nodded. "You knew about the pin?"

"Of course," Jack said giving her a sideways look, "...and we know Bronson tried to pawn it...without the stones. It's not looking good for the two of them."

Lexy felt a bubble of happiness. She had found the killer! Or killers. Either way, the case would be solved and she could get paid. Most importantly, Jack didn't seem mad at her.

"I'll have to get the paperwork rolling, we'll need warrants and statements if we want to bring them in tomorrow. That could take all nigh-" He broke off the last word and looked at Lexy.

She cocked an eyebrow at him. "What?"

"We were supposed to go out on a date tonight." He said.

Lexy felt her stomach drop. She knew what was coming next. If they went on their date, he might not get the paperwork done. She wasn't sure which she wanted more.

Jack put his hands on her shoulders. "You're more important to me than this job. I can fill out paperwork tomorrow and bring them in for questioning the next day."

Lexy looked into his honey brown eyes, warmth spreading through her body. She *wanted* to go out with Jack, but, on the other hand Candice was packing - tomorrow could be too late.

"I have an idea." She reached up and played with his collar. "Maybe you could do the paperwork tonight, and then...when it is done...come by my house for a nightcap." *Skip the date and go straight to the good stuff.*

Jack smiled, pulling her close. "That sounds like a very good idea." He lowered his lips to hers making Lexy forget all about murderers, bakery equipment and overdue bills if only for a few, delightful seconds.

Chapter Sixteen

Lexy padded into the kitchen, her bare feet making slapping sounds on the linoleum. The sun streaming through the window lit up the room. She smiled when she saw Jack's coffee cup neatly placed in the sink, a warm glow of contentment filling her.

She felt happier than she had in weeks. Soon the killer would be behind bars, she'd get the payment she needed for the bakery and her and Jack were back together. What more could she ask for?

Sprinkles happily danced at her feet. She squatted to pet her. "It's a beautiful day today, what do you say we go visit Nans, then take a walk in the woods to retrieve your leash?"

Sprinkles increased the pace of her dancing, Lexy didn't know if that was a yes to the walk or a sign the dog was hungry. She filled her ceramic dog bowl, setting it on the floor.

While Sprinkles munched contentedly on her dog food, Lexy scrounged in the fridge for breakfast.

She ignored the eggs, milk and fruit reaching straight for a small banana cream pie she had stashed in the back. She figured it was the closest thing to a balanced breakfast because it had fruit from the bananas, protein from the cream and carbs from the crust.

While she ate the pie, she rummaged in the drawers for Sprinkles's old leash. The new one, an expensive retractible model was still tangled in the woods and Lexy needed something for her visit to Nans. Sprinkles was good at staying with her - unless a cat or squirrel wandered into view - but she still wanted to make sure the dog was safe and didn't wander around the retirement center unattended.

She saw the frayed material of the old purple leash shoved in the back of a drawer, grabbing it with her fingertips, she pulled it out. It was beaten almost to shreds with some very thin areas, but it would have to do. She shoved it in her purse, than headed upstairs to shower and change.

***

"Sprinkles!" Ida shouted the dogs name from the other side of the Retirement Center lobby. Sprinkles wagged her tail, straining at the end of the leash - she couldn't get over to greet the four women fast enough.

Lexy let the dog pull her towards them, then perched on a chair while the older women lavished Sprinkles with attention.

"Are you going to bring her around to the other residents?" Ruth asked as she bent forward to stroke the dogs ears.

Lexy occasionally brought Sprinkles to the Retirement Center to visit some of the elderly patients who couldn't get out, she was always a big hit. "Not today," Lexy said, "I'm in a bit of a hurry but I wanted to stop by and tell you some big news about the case."

The four ladies switched their attention from the dog, sitting up in their seats they stared at Lexy expectantly.

"I found the killer!"

Lexy heard four sharp gasps. She saw eight wrinkly eyes narrow. Four grayish blue heads bent forward across the table.

"Well...who is it?" Helen asked.

"Candice."

"Candice?" Nans, Ruth, Helen and Ida echoed in unison.

Lexy nodded, then told them all about the previous days events. "She's probably at the station being arrested right now...and maybe even Bronson too."

"That's fabulous! Another case solved by the Ladies Detective Club." The other ladies nodded in agreement.

Solved by the Ladies Detective Club? Lexy wrinkled her brow thinking she had done most of the work.

"Now dear, don't give us that look. Sure, we sent you off to do all the legwork, but we did do the investigation to find out who pawned the brooch."

"And eliminated the people from Texas and Trixie as suspects when we found they had alibis," Ida added.

"And pushed you in the right direction," Nans said with a firm shake of her head. "Of course, we couldn't have done it without you, though." The others nodded their agreement.

"Yes, Lexy, nice work," Ruth said. "But I wonder-*why* would Candice want to murder Chastine?"

Lexy chewed on her lip. That *was* a good question, of all the suspects, Candice was the one without a motive. "She probably was in on it with Bronson. He had a pretty good motive with Chastine on the brink of marrying into family money."

Ruth tilted her head apparently thinking about Lexy's theory.

"Well, I just wanted to stop by to let you know the good news. Sprinkles and I are heading back to the walking trail. It's such a beautiful day...and I need to retrieve her leash. It got tangled in the vines yesterday and we had to leave it to run off and follow Bronson. It was expensive, and this leash won't last much longer." She held up the frayed end of the purple leash.

Lexy got up, hugging Nans she bid the other women a good day, then she picked up Sprinkles and headed out the door.

Emerging from the building into the warm sunshine made her feel like singing. Everything was going her way - it was a beautiful day and soon her life would return to normal. For the first time in weeks she felt relaxed, looking forward to the future. Nothing could possibly go wrong now.

Chapter Seventeen

"When we find those shoes, we'll have the evidence we need so you might as well confess now and save us all some trouble."

Jack sat across the table from Candice, who squirmed in her hard metal chair. Jack could see her eyes starting to fill with tears, her hands were clasped in her lap but he could see them trembling. She hung her head.

"I…didn't…kill…her." She said softly.

"I think the evidence says otherwise. If the DNA on your shoe matches Chastine's, and the stones in your ring are from her brooch, then I'd say we have the case locked up." Jack almost felt sorry for the girl, she didn't seem like a killer, but then he'd met quite a few who didn't. He suspected, however, that she didn't act alone and he wanted to nail the accomplice too.

Jack stood up. Putting his palms flat on the table he leaned across it, his face close to Candice's. "We could go a lot easier on you if you tell us who helped you."

Candice looked up, he could see the fear in her eyes. *She's afraid of the other person.*

He started pacing around the room, trying to find an angle, a wedge he could use to get her to tell him the truth.

"The thing is, we can't figure out *why* you did it. If someone forced you to do it, or you were an unwitting accomplice, you might get off if you tell us who the other person was." He spun around to see if she would take the bait. She remained silent, he could almost see the wheels turning in her mind, trying to figure a way out. They were always like this at first, but it never worked out the way they hoped.

A light tap on the door made Candice jump out of her seat.

"I'll be back in a few minutes." Jack opened the door a crack and slid out into the hall. On the other side, John Darling was leaning against the wall, leafing through a file.

"Did you get the lab results back from the shoes?"

"No, but I have Bronson Toliver in the other room. He seemed quite agitated when I told him we were also holding Candice. He denies having anything to do with killing Chastine."

Jack glanced through the small window in the doorway into the other interrogation room. Bronson sat straight backed in the chair, his finger tapping nervously on the top of the table.

"Let's see if I can get anything out of him," Jack opened the door. He walked over to the table, letting the door slam behind him. Pulling out the chair opposite Bronson, he turned it around and straddled it, sitting facing Bronson with his arms leaning against the back of the chair.

"We've looked at your files - we know you have a violent past, why don't you just tell us what happened. What did you kill her with, and where is it?"

"I have no idea what you are talking about." Bronson said the words calmly, but the twitch in his jaw let Jack know he was anything but calm.

Jack tried another tactic. "How did you get Candice to go along with you?"

"Candice? What's she got to do with it?"

"We know you pawned the brooch and her ring has the same stone in it. Those stones are laser inscribed with a serial number. My guy is working on tracing the number right now - I bet it leads us straight back to Chastine's brooch." Jack saw a look of genuine surprise flicker in Bronson's eyes.

"That doesn't prove either one of us murdered her."

"No, but we have a pair of shoes from Candice's condo with blood all over them...when the tests come back from the lab proving it's Chastine's blood...well," Jack shrugged, "that's as good as a confession."

Jack stood up. Turning the chair back around, he dragged it to the table. He walked towards the door, then turned, looking straight at Bronson. "Once we have her nailed, we'll offer her a deal to turn you in. If she does, her testimony along with your violent record and Blake's testimony will put you away for a long time...even if we never do find the murder weapon."

Jack saw Bronson's eyebrows knit together. "Blake's testimony?"

"Yes, according to Blake..." Jack took his notebook out and flipped through a few pages. "He saw you coming up the stairs at 2:30 in the morning. The time of death is listed as 2:15 so the timing would be perfect for you to kill her, hide the murder weapon, rip her brooch off her blouse and then skulk up the stairs to your room."

Bronson bolted out of his seat, Jack saw anger flash in his eyes. "Blake said that?"

Jack made a show of looking at his notes again. "That's what it says."

"That...little...liar. That's not true--it was the other way around. *I* was in my room and saw *him* coming up the stairs at 2:30 in the morning.

***

Jack leaned against the door in the hallway. *So Bronson was trying to point the finger at Blake...interesting.*

He looked down at the folder in his hands - inside was everything he needed to nail Candice for the murder. Hopefully once he confronted her with it, she'd try to get a lighter sentence by telling him exactly what happened and they'd be able to use her testimony to prosecute Bronson.

Jack opened the door to the room Candice was in. Stepping inside, he slapped the folder down on the table.

"The DNA results from your shoes are in here," He tapped his index finger on the folder, "guess what it says."

He saw Candice's face go white.

"Oh, and another interesting thing. We tracked down the serial number on the diamond - you know the one you ripped out of the brooch? It was originally purchased by a Bob McCafferty to be custom made into that brooch. We discovered Mr. McCafferty is the former fiancee of Chastine." Jack saw a flicker of recognition in her eyes so he moved in for the kill.

"I know you didn't do it alone, so my offer is still open - tell me who was in on it with you, and I'll see you get a reduced sentence. My money is on Bronson." He saw Candice stiffen at Bronson's name.

"Why? Do you have some evidence on Bronson?"

"We may have him tied to the murder weapon." Jack knew his lie had hit it's mark when he saw a look of confusion cross her face.

She shook her head. "No, you can't."

"No? He pawned the brooch *and* he was seen coming up the stairs shortly after the murder occurred. Where were you, still downstairs with the body?"

"Who saw him?"

"Blake."

Jack saw Candice's face crumble, she sagged in her chair. A tear slipped down each cheek. Jack handed her a tissue.

"Are you ready to talk yet? We have enough evidence to take this to court and you *will* go to jail unless you can clear yourself."

Candice nodded, sniffling into a tissue. "Bronson didn't have anything to do with the murder...it was Blake."

***

Jack felt a jolt of shock. *Blake?* His eyes narrowed. He motioned at the two way mirror for

John to come in with the appropriate papers to take a statement.

"So, the three of you were in on it together?" He saw Candice's eyes grow wide.

"No!"

Jack lifted his brows. "There's certainly enough evidence to suggest it. Why don't you tell us your side of the story?"

John had settled in a chair at the end of the table, a tape recorder next to the paperwork in front of him. Jack heard the metallic click and hiss of the tape recorder starting up.

Candice swiped at her eyes with the tissue. "I was at the house visiting Bronson that night."

"At two in the morning?" Jack's brows knit together.

He saw Candice's cheeks turn pink. "Yes...we were lovers."

"Go on."

"We didn't want anyone to know...we didn't want any trouble because I was Chastine's assistant. We hadn't been dating very long, it was actually the first time I had been in his room at the mansion..."

Jack nodded.

"Anyway, I couldn't stay all night, so I snuck down the back stairs to leave through the kitchen."

"What time was this?"

"It was at 2:15 - I remember because it takes me fifteen minutes to get home from there and I remember thinking I could be in bed by 2:30."

"Only you didn't get home at 2:30, did you?"

She shook her head. "No. Blake must have heard me coming down the stairs. When I came out in the kitchen the first thing I saw was Chastine's body...and all that blood." Jack saw her shiver.

"And you just walked over it and went home? You didn't scream or call for help?"

"Like I said, Blake must have heard me. He grabbed me from behind when I walked out into the room. He covered my mouth before I even had a chance to scream."

"You expect us to believe that? Why wouldn't you turn him in? And why would you protect him all this time, when you knew we had evidence against *you*?"

Jack saw Candice's eyes start to get moist again, he reached for more tissues but she waved him away. "It wasn't like that. Blake threatened me. He kept the knife and said he would use it to frame me for the murder if I said anything."

"Sorry Candice, it just doesn't add up. It would just be his word against yours in that case. I don't see why you would keep quiet. Unless he had something else on you...like you were an accessory in the murder."

Candice looked down at her hands. "He *did* have something else on me. . But it wasn't that I helped him kill her."

Jack spread his hands. "Care to clue us in?"

Candice looked up. "Bob McCafferty - the man who bought the diamond? He's my father."

The room was silent. Now it was all starting to make sense.

"Your father was engaged to Chastine back in Texas and she broke his heart, so you came here to kill her."

Candice shook her head. "No! Not to kill her, to get even with her. To break up her relationship with Xavier. My father is a bitter, beaten man now because of what she did to him - I wanted to make her suffer, to make sure she didn't get to live happily ever after with anyone else's millions. But I would never kill her. I'm no murderer." She looked pleadingly at Jack. "You have to believe me."

Jack narrowed his eyes. "If she was engaged to your father, why didn't she recognize you?"

"We'd actually never met. I was overseas when she met my dad. By the time I got back to the states, she'd already dumped him."

"So where does Blake come in?"

"Somehow he had found out who I really was. Why he wouldn't have said anything before, I have no idea. He's sneaky like that - always trying to dig up dirt on people so he can hold it against them at the right time." Jack saw a look of disgust cross her face. "Anyway, he said I had the perfect motive for killing Chastine so if I told on him, he'd simply plant the weapon in my condo and point the finger at me."

"So you kept his dirty secret."

She looked down at her hands and nodded. "I didn't want to go to jail for murder and I also didn't want Bronson to find out I was lying to him about who I was."

"And the blood on your shoes?"

Candice face turned beet red. "After I got over the shock of what I had discovered, I have to admit, I wasn't too upset she was dead. I took a closer look - just to make sure. That's when I noticed she was wearing the brooch Dad had given her. She always wore it - every day. It was like a big slap in the face to see it on her. So, I leaned over and ripped it off her blouse. I guess I must have stepped in some blood when I did."

Jack exchanged a look with John. *Was she telling the truth or making up an elaborate lie to get away with murder?*

"And then what?" Jack prodded.

"Nothing," she said, "I ran out the back door and got away from there as fast as I could."

She looked up at Jack, pleadingly. "Bronson didn't have anything to do with the murder - you *have* to let him go."

Jack motioned with his head for John to meet him out in the hall. He stood, looking down at Candice. "Thanks for your statement, we'll have to do some checking and talk to the DA about your involvement. For now, you can stay in here - I don't think we need to put you in a cell...just yet."

He saw her face relax, more tears threatened to make an appearance. "Thank you," she said.

Jack opened the door for John, stepping out into the hall behind him.

"What do you think?" John asked.

"For all we know, she made up the whole story *with* Bronson to frame Blake. We need to bring him in and see if he changes his story or we can catch him in a lie."

"What about Bronson?"

"We don't have much to hold him on...let's try to keep him as long as we can. He could be mixed up in this and I'd hate to see him get away. We'll hold him until his lawyer starts screaming. In the mean time, let's get the paperwork started to bring in Blake."

Chapter Eighteen

"Isn't it a wonderful day, Sprinkles?" Lexy stretched her arms up to the sun. Grabbing the end of Sprinkles's leash, she headed down the path.

The sun's rays filtered through the tree trunks causing slices of light to permeate the woods. Like the day before, the friendly chirping of birds and the crunching of footsteps on dry leaves was all that could be heard.

"Now where is your other leash?" Lexy asked out loud, keeping a close eye on the area to the left of the path. "Oh, there it is!"

She let go of Sprinkles's leash. Bending down, she worked the knots with her fingers, trying carefully not to break a nail. Glancing up she noticed the path was only about 50 feet away from the Toliver property where they were building the new cabana. She felt an icy shiver walk up her spine thinking of the murder which had happened there not even a week ago. She felt grateful Bronson was in custody so she wouldn't have to worry about running into him.

Finally working the leash free, she looked around for Sprinkles. Realizing with a start the dog had wandered off, she scanned the woods, then saw her, over by the property line, making her way towards the Toliver's yard.

Lexy started off towards her. She was about to call out to the little dog when a sudden movement in the Toliver's yard caught her eye. It was Blake. *What is he doing over there?* He was over by the area where the fresh cement had just been poured. He was balancing on the edge of a form, looking down in.

Sprinkles saw Blake too and gave an excited yip, taking off at a trot towards him. The fence dividing that part of the yard from the nature preserve had been taken down for the construction allowing the dog to bound onto the Toliver's property. The little dog was such a socialite, she'd run over to any stranger to get attention. *I hope Blake likes dogs.*

Instead of happily greeting the dog like most people did, Blake jerked his head up at the noise. His eyes scanned the woods and met Lexy's. Lexy's stomach churned when she saw the look of malice in his eyes. That was not the flirty, fun Blake she knew.

Then a sharp beam of sunlight glinting off something in his hand caught her eye. Lexy felt her heart turn to ice when she realized what it was - her seven inch serrated knife. The knife that had killed Chastine.

***

"What are you doing?" Lexy heard the words come out of her mouth before she could think better of saying them.

"You!" He pointed at her with the knife. "Nosy bitch...are you spying on me?"

"No..." Lexy shook her head. *Should she try to play nice?* It was too late to pretend she didn't see the knife. Lexy's head swam, adrenalin coursed through her body. Her first instinct was to turn and run, but Sprinkles was over near Blake. She needed to grab the dog and get the hell out of there.

"Sprinkles, come!" Her voice came out an octave higher than usual, giving away the panic she felt in her chest.

A second later, she realized she shouldn't have called to the dog. Blake turned, looking at Sprinkles, then jumped to the patio and scooped the dog up, holding the knife at her throat.

"You wouldn't want me to hurt your dog, would you?"

Lexy shook her head, icy fingers squeezed her heart.

"Then come over here."

Lexy felt frozen in place, her instincts were screaming at her to run, but she couldn't let him hurt Sprinkles. She forced her legs to move.

He kept talking as she got closer. "You know, Lexy, I really liked you. It's too bad you had to keep sticking your nose into this. Coming over and poking around. Combing the dumpster."

Lexy's eyebrows raised in surprise.

"Yes, that was me watching you from the house. I know you were looking for this," he raised the knife up, "but I had it hidden well."

Lexy had picked her way over to him. She was standing about five feet away.

"Closer!" He pressed the knife into Sprinkles. The dog gave a yelp which made Lexy's stomach clench.

"Please don't hurt her!" Lexy moved closer to him.

"I won't hurt her if you do what I say." He grabbed her arm roughly, shoving her through the door to the cabana.

He kicked the door shut then spun her around. "I'm going to regret having to do this," he said, tracing the tip of the knife from the top of her throat all the way down her chest stopping just where her bra started. "Everything would have been okay, if you had just minded our own business. We might have even had some fun together." He released her arm and she stumbled backwards.

"You killed Chastine?"

Blake snorted. "Yep. When they brought Candice and Bronson in today, I had the perfect plan to frame them, but now you've put a kink in the plan. Regrettably, I will have to straighten out that kink." He lifted the knife again.

"But why?" Lexy hoped if she kept him talking it would buy her some time to think of a way to get free.

Blake walked over to the corner. Bending down, he came up with a length of thick rope in one hand while still holding Sprinkles in the other.

He turned and walked towards Lexy. "You wanna know why? I guess I can tell you since you won't be around to tell anyone else." He hefted the rope in one hand, then put Sprinkles down, still holding the end of her leash. The little dog tugged at the end to try to get to Lexy. Lexy winced as Blake roughly jerked her back.

"Chastine and I were lovers...before she took up with Dad. Once she found out how much money he had, she went after him like a greyhound after a rabbit. The only problem was, she still wanted me on the side. Normally, I don't care how many other guys a woman has...but when the other guy is your own father, well, *that's* too disgusting even for me." He made a face.

Lexy nodded to encourage him to continue, Sprinkles strained at the leash, the frayed section getting even thinner.

"I wanted to break it off. She wouldn't let me - threatened to take away all the money once she was married to dad. That night she had requested a *rendezvous,*" he said the word with a look of distaste on his face. "I left the front door open for her and we met in the kitchen. We argued. Things got out of hand. Before I knew it, I was standing over her body holding a bloody knife."

Blake shrugged. "And now I guess I'm going to have to use that knife again," he said, taking a step towards Lexy.

Sprinkles strained even harder. The leash snapped. The dog broke free, running to Lexy's side.

"Run, Sprinkles!" She commanded. Blake lunged at her, grabbing her by the hair, jerking her head backwards.

Sprinkles didn't run, she leaped for Blake's ankles, sinking her teeth in and barking loudly.

Blake tried to throw the dog off. Kicking out his feet, he lost his balance. His grip on Lexy's hair loosened. She spun around raising her knee hard. She felt it connect with soft flesh, heard a grunt and saw Blake collapse in a ball on the floor.

Lexy grabbed the barking dog and ran for the door.

"Come back - bitch!" She heard Blake's heavy footsteps behind her.

Picking up speed, she wrenched the door open, catapulting herself forward, trying to put as much distance between her and Blake as possible.

Her stiletto heel caught on a hole in the flooring, her heart stopped as she was jerked off balance. She felt herself falling. She clutched Sprinkles even closer bracing for the hard impact of the ground.

Instead, she felt strong arms circle her waist, pulling her upright. She tensed, ready to fight Blake off with everything she had, then looked up...right into the eyes of Jack Perillo.

***

A blur of activity was going on behind her. People were shouting and running. She turned in time to see John Darling leap onto Blake and bring him crashing to the ground. The knife skittered across the driveway. Someone bent to retrieve it.

"That's the knife that murdered Chastine!" Lexy pointed at it.

"Bag that knife for evidence," Jack yelled, then, putting his finger under Lexy's chin he turned her head back to face him.

"Lexy, what the *hell* are you doing here?"

Lexy winced at the anger in his voice. She took a step back from Jack, cuddling Sprinkles closer, stroking the dogs fur.

"I didn't actually come *here*," she said. "I was walking Sprinkles on the walking trails over there when I saw Blake with the knife. I think he was trying to get rid of it in the new cement." She pointed towards the cement forms in front of the cabana.

"Anyway, Blake knew I saw him. He forced me into the cabana. He confessed - he's the one who murdered Chastine!" She said, feeling a little sheepish since she was the one who had insisted it was Candice.

"He confessed? Well that saves us a lot of time. Candice said she had stumbled onto the murder scene and he was blackmailing her to keep quiet."

"Blackmailing her?"

"Yes, it turns out Candice was the daughter of Chastine's former fiancee - I guess she had quite a grudge against her. Blake found that out and threatened to reveal her secret and frame her for the murder. That's why he still had the knife."

"And Bronson?"

"According to Candice he had no idea about any of this."

"How did you know we were back here?" Lexy asked.

"We pulled up in front with a warrant to bring Blake in. When we heard Sprinkles barking back here, we figured something was going on." Jack reached down to ruffle the fur behind Sprinkles ears.

"I guess you might have saved me twice today, girl." Lexy kissed the top of the dogs head, then placed her gently on the ground. "Sprinkles bit Blake's leg when he grabbed me - it was because if her I was able to get away. Thank God you came when you did, or he might have caught up to me." Lexy felt a shiver run up her spine.

Jack looked down at the little dog. "Sprinkles is going to get a big treat tonight," he said, then he looked back at Lexy, his eyes turning serious. "I'm just glad Blake didn't hurt you...this is why I didn't want you investigating any of this. I couldn't bear it if something happened to you."

Lexy felt her heart melt. "I know, I'm sorry. I only wanted to help find the killer so I could get paid."

Jack put his hands on Lexy's shoulders. Bending down, he brushed his lips against her forehead, then pulled her in for a hug. "I guess I'm going to have to spend a lot more time with you from now on in order to keep you out of trouble."

Lexy smiled up at him. "I'll be looking forward to that, Detective Perillo."

Epilogue

"To murder!" Jack raised his cut crystal wine glass for a toast, the light from the chandeliers overhead reflecting off the glass in brilliant sparks of light.

"Murder?" John asked from across the table. "That's a funny thing to toast to."

"Well, if it wasn't for murder, we all might not be sitting here together tonight."

It was true, Lexy thought, looking around the table. Chastine's murder had brought her and Jack back together and the investigation had caused John and Cassie to keep bumping into each other in a way that never would have happened otherwise.

"Here, here." She said, raising her glass. The four wine glasses met in the middle of the table. Wine sloshed as they clinked together, the sound drowned out only by the laughter of the people holding the glasses.

Lexy felt the contented, warm glow of happiness which comes when things are going just right. She looked around the table. The fine linen, fancy china and glittering silver were nice to look at, but nothing compared to her four best friends who she shared the table with.

Jack was to her left, John Darling to her right and Cassie across from her. Behind Cassie, she could see the lights from the restaurant sparkle on the water of the falls. She looked down at her plate of prime rib, garlic mashed and green beans and felt truly blessed.

"Did you guys hear? It looks like there is going to be a wedding after all!" Lexy said excitedly.

Across the table she saw Cassie's eyes grow wide, darting from Lexy's face to her left hand.

Lexy laughed, "Not me, silly. Xavier Toliver! He's going to marry Trixie and, the best part is, he's hired us to do the catering, so we'll get all the money we need for the kitchen equipment after all!"

"That's wonderful!" Cassie said, then turning to Jack she asked, "What's going to happen to Candice, now?"

"She'll probably get off with just a slap. She wasn't actually involved in the murder and Bronson has hired the best lawyers to represent her."

"Well, I'm just glad we caught the real killer *and* he'll be spending a lot of time in jail. It turns out he was always the bad boy - not Bronson like everyone thought. In fact, Bronson took the fall for quite a few of the things Blake did." John said.

"I'm glad Bronson and Candice ended up together. She's kind of nice once you get to know her. I hear she moved into the Toliver mansion. There may be a second wedding in the works." Lexy winked at Cassie "I hope we get the catering job for that one too."

"*I'm* glad the whole thing is solved and you girls won't have to put yourselves in danger by investigating any more murders." Jack slid a sideways glance at Lexy.

Lexy smiled at him above a forkful of potatoes. She thought about the investigation. Sure, it *was* a bit dangerous, but she liked putting together the clues and it was fun working with Nans and the Ladies Detective Club. In fact, the ladies had asked her to help them out with a few other mysteries they had on their plate. She was considering it, this investigation stuff was kind of a fun hobby.

"Right, Lexy?" She looked up to see Jack looking at her with his brows raised.

"What?"

"You won't be getting involved in any more murder investigations, right?" Jack prodded.

"Oh, right," she said. Focusing her attention on her steak, she deftly avoided eye contact, not that she was lying or anything. She didn't plan to get involved in any more murder investigations...at least not *tonight*.

The End.

***

Lexy's Danish Pastry Recipe

Don't you just love the flaky, buttery taste of Danish pastry? Lexy says one of the keys is to keep the butter ice cold. Here's her recipe for making Danish pastry from scratch:

Recipe makes 16 Danish pastries

Pastry Dough

Ingredients:

1/2 ounce active dry yeast (this is 2 1/4 ounce packages or 5 tablespoons)
1 teaspoon salt
1/2 cup sugar
3 egg yolks
1 teaspoon almond extract
1 teaspoon vanilla extract
2/3 cup milk
3 3/4 cups flour
3 sticks unsalted butter, cut into small chunks

Preparation:

Proof the yeast in 1/4 cup warm water for 5 min. Once it is foamy, stir in the salt, sugar, egg yolks, almond extract, vanilla extract and milk. Add 3 1/4 cups of the flour. Stir until the dough is slightly sticky, then cover and put in the fridge for 1 hour.

On a very cold surface (a marble pastry board works best), combine the butter and 1/2 cup of the flour, then roll out into a 6" square. Work quickly so the butter does not get too soft. Wrap the square in plastic wrap and put it in the fridge for 30 minutes or long enough so that it is firm but still pliable (not so cold that it breaks when you handle it).

Turn the dough out onto a well floured surface and roll it into a 12" square. Place the butter in the middle. Pull in the corners of the dough to the middle so that you are encasing the butter inside the dough (this is what makes it flaky). The entire butter piece should be covered and your dough should look like an envelope. Seal the edges of the dough by pinching them together then flatten gently with a rolling pin. Roll it out gently to an 18" x 18" piece of dough.

Fold the top quarter of the dough into the middle and the bottom quarter to the middle so the two pieces meet. Then fold those over each other so that you have a piece that kind of looks like a book.

Roll it out again into an 18" square and fold again. Wrap in plastic and chill for 1 hour.

Repeat the rolling, folding and chilling process two more times.

Chill the dough overnight.

To create the Pastries:

Preheat oven to 350F.

Roll the chilled dough to a 1/4" thickness.

You can cut the dough into squares of 4 inches each. Stretch the corners and put about 1 tablespoon of filling in the middle. Then fold the corners over the filling to form a flap.

OR, you can cut the dough into 1" strips, then twist them and roll into a round spiral. Place the filling in the middle of the spiral.

For filling, you can use any type of fruit preserve, or go with the cheese Danish filling recipe provided below.

Brush the dough with egg wash.

Bake on lightly greased baking sheets for about 30 min. or until they are golden brown.

Drizzle with the glaze.

Glaze

Ingredients:

1 cup confectioners sugar
2 tablespoons lemon juice

Preparation:

Slowly add the lemon juice to the confectioners sugar until you have a pourable glaze. You don't want it to be too thin or it won't make lines on the danish. Too thick and it won't pour.

Cheese Danish Filling

Ingredients:

8 ounces cream cheese
1 teaspoon vanilla
1/2 cup sugar
2 egg yolks (at room temperature)
1/2 teaspoon lemon zest
pinch salt

Preparation:

Cream the cream cheese and sugar together either by hand or using a mixer on low.

Add the rest of the ingredients and mix until combined - don't overmix!

Easy Danish Pastry

Making pastry dough can be a bit difficult. Lexy has a commercial kitchen and years of experience at her disposal, but if you don't .. and you want to make some quick pastry dough, here's an easy method:

Ingredients:

1 Box of puff pastry
Filling of your choice
1 egg
1 tablespoon water

Preparation:

Preheat oven to 400(f)

Unfold a sheet of puff pastry onto a floured board.

Roll it out until it is 10" square.

Cut the sheet into 4 equal squares.

Put 1 tablespoon of filling in the middle of each square.

Beat the egg together with the tablespoon of water to make an egg wash.

Brush the egg wash on the edges of the pastry.

Pull the two corners of the pastry in and pinch together. Repeat with the other two corners so that the filling is enclosed in the pastry.

Brush the egg wash on the outside of the dough.

Repeat to make as many pastries as you want.

Refrigerate the pastries for 15 minutes.

Bake for 20 minutes, or until they turn golden brown.

A Note From The Author

Thanks for buying my book - I hope you enjoyed reading it as much as I enjoyed writing it! I love the characters in this series and strive to make the books a fun read that helps you relax after a hard day.

If you liked the book and feel inclined to leave a review or tell your friends, it would be much appreciated!

Also, I **love** to talk to my fans and you can communicate with me on my Facebook fanpage or through twitter:

http://www.facebook.com/leighanndobbsbooks

http://twitter.com/leighanndobbs

Don't forget to signup to receive notifications of new book releases and cool contests here:

http://www.leighanndobbs.com/news

I would never share your email address with anyone and I promise not to inundate you with emails - I only send them when I release a new book or have a new contest where you can win cool stuff (you never have to buy anything to win). I typically only send an email once every couple of weeks.

Finally, this book has been edited many times over. I've used several types of software, read it over many times, my husband has read it and I've paid a professional editor to edit it. In the end though, we are only human so there might be a few mistakes we all missed - if you find one, please feel free to email me at lee@leighanndobbs.com and let me know! Thanks!

About Me:

Leighann Dobbs is the pen name of an author who lives in New Hampshire with her husband, their trusty Chihuahua mix Mojo and beautiful rescue cat, Kitty. She likes to write romance and cozy mystery novelettes perfect for the busy person on the go. These stories are great for someone who doesn't have a lot of time for reading a full novel. Why not pick one up and escape to another time and place the next time you are waiting for an appointment, enjoying a bath or waiting to pick up the kids at soccer?

Find out about her latest books at:

http://www.leighanndobbs.com/newsletter/

CPSIA information can be obtained
at www.ICGtesting.com
Printed in the USA
LVHW082004170420
653851LV00019B/1711